Grounds

PAULINE HALL

GROUNDS

BRANDON

First published 1983
Brandon Book Publishers Ltd
Dingle, Co. Kerry, Ireland

*This book is published with the financial assistance of the Arts Council/
An Chomhairle Ealaíon, Ireland.
Typesetting & Makeup: Gifford & Craven, Dublin
Printed by Biddles Ltd, Guildford, England*

for Catherine

I

ONCE, FAR BACK, there was a whole song, and men's voices on the radio.

'From Tobruk down the road to Alamein'.

That line alone endured, the names always thrilling and comforting, a private treat for when Margaret was in bed, in the time before she saw the dummy at the RDS.

The dummy was something like a person, but with no face, all khaki cloth gathered clumsily at the wrists and ankles. Its head fell sideways as it swung, an object of menace, dumb and boneless. If Margaret took her eyes off the coats hanging behind the door, they turned into the dummy when she looked back. So not for anything would she let her glance wander to the three linked shapes, the stains on the ceiling that were God the Father, God the Son and God the Holy Ghost. When a car turned outside, the lights raked across the walls and ceiling. She never quite caught what the shape behind the door looked like, as she was too scared to look then. If Dada came in, dropped by the car that had lit up her room, she would hear his voice (slower than usual, nearly all on one note) and Mama's brisker tones. The door might be shut quite hard on those nights when Mama stayed up late. Margaret listened as they came past the door of her room. She always hoped that they might have some reason to come in, but their different treads — her light, skipping step and his solid planting of the feet — went on past her door to their own room, beside Dutch's.

After the house was again filled up with silence, Margaret thought out what she had to do. There were two bad bits: the short one was the dash to the door, keeping as far as possible away from the shape hanging on the back. Then, listening for a moment to the hushed house and her own heart, she got ready for the long bad bit: the dash across the landing to Dutch's room.

A strange smell that was like nothing else in the house went with the dull pink walls. Pink too was the eiderdown that covered Dutch's large shape in the bed. Margaret lifted the corner and felt the way the mattress was raised because Dutch's weight had dragged down the middle.

"I can't sleep, I've really tried." Dutch made her peculiar swallow.

"Why can you not sleep, chicken?"

"I hate going to sleep. It's like dying. Because of the prayer: 'If I die before I wake'."

"All right. Get into the snuggy."

When she put her freezing feet against Dutch and sheltered close to her back, sleep would be just upon her.

Dutch hoped to help her brother's daughter to sleep by herself. She took the big picture of the Sacred Heart from beside her own wardrobe and put it into Margaret's room. As she looked at where it was propped against the wall Margaret felt it was out of place. It belonged with Dutch's things: the crucifix with the steps at the base, the photos in identical brown frames of Dutch and her cousin Martin from Boston, the bag of golf clubs and the drawing of de Valera.

Even when it was too dark to see, Margaret could remember what Holy God looked like. In the picture his mous-

[8]

tache and beard were silky and neatly parted, his mouth
and nose as perfectly shaped as a doll's. Over his breast
the blue robe was slit open to show his heart, ringed with
thorns, wounded and seeping blood, smoking even with
the ardour of his love.

"To show that he's always close to good children,"
Dutch explained, "his eyes will always follow you, no matter
what part of the room you're in."

Margaret didn't understand how it could be so, but even
when she tried standing flat against the wall, beside the picture, she felt the clear blue gaze fixed on her. She considered
turning the picture to the wall but didn't dare. Many more
nights came when she raced across the landing, and Dutch
never refused to take her in.

Carmel put her apron down on the kitchen table where she
had her meals. When she was ready, one foot on the ground,
one on the pedal, Mama lifted Margaret onto the little seat at
the back of the bicycle. The whole road opened up in front
of her as they went to school. The house with the dentist's
plate was guarded by two stone lions, like the castle in Jack
the Giant Killer but these were toothless. At the turn in the
road a wine-coloured door had the name printed in gold: she
hated to miss that, or the fat cockers that stood at the gate of
a garden without grass, a stretch of gravel and stone-ringed
flower beds.

Miss Ackroyd, who was to teach her, had a rather fierce
red face and white hair covered with a net which held it in
against her ears like headphones. She hauled one large ban-
daged foot onto a stool in front of her, and her movements
were awkward. She banged her stick on the floor if the
whispering got too loud.

The story she read them was about a Princess of Tyre
who was bathing in the sea and happened to step upon a
certain kind of shell. Crushed by her foot, the shell gave out
a purple dye which became the royal colour of that country
and was bought by merchants all over the world. The cover
of the history book was purple. Though there were other
stories in it that Margaret liked — for one, the story of

Blondel the musician finding his master King Richard the Lion-Hearted in prison — for her the book was above all a piece of marvellous purple cloth come down from that first beach.

The teachers were careful to bring her out to do sums whenever they were studying the Bible. She never knew what went on at the Bible classes, so when she had to go to the toilet one summer day, she detoured on her way back to her sums lesson so as to pass that classroom. The window was open and, stooping down, she opened and then began to fasten the strap of her sandal. It somehow surprised her to hear Walter's voice, usually indistinct and sniffly, now strong and stirring.

"You come to me with a sword and shield and a javelin, but I come to you in the name of the Lord of Hosts."

Margaret felt the skin on her scalp crawl: a feeling strange and lovely. Walter was a dirty, smelly boy. No-one ever wanted to sit beside him; they copied Daphne, who shrank away, remembering how, the first day, he had spilled milk on her dark brown slacks.

At tea Margaret asked: "Why don't I go to Bible classes with the others?"

"Because they're Protestants and you're a Catholic," Mama told her.

"I think I'd prefer to be a Protestant."

Margaret went onto the step, into the sunshine. Carmel washed the tiles every morning, twisting the grey cloth into a thick worm over the bucket.

One small pane in the halldoor was edged with putty, not lead like the others; Margaret fingered its bumpy line. Patricia Murphy had thrown a Dinky car at William, and Margaret remembered the sound of metal and glass in sudden collision. Patricia's mother had been most apologetic but they had never matched the colour of that pane.

That same summer, Dutch and Mama began to talk of sending her to another school. "She should be starting to prepare for her First Holy Communion, and she's old enough now to go to Miss Dillon's with Patricia Murphy on the bus."

Patricia Murphy could not believe what Margaret told her about her first school. "You couldn't have gone there!"

On Serpentine Avenue one day, with Patricia Murphy, she passed Walter. They looked at each other, then said a kind of surprised hello.

"Who is he?" asked Patricia.

"Walter. I used to go to school with him."

"How did you stick it? I bet you're glad you changed."

It was probably Walter's clothes that had put Patricia off; he wore a long belted coat like a man and heavy boots.

They reminded Margaret of the boots the orphans wore. She had first seen the orphans one smoky November evening, advancing like a file of soldiers through the dusk. They were all in grey, with knee-length shorts of some rough material, grey jerseys with collars and three buttons. Their haircuts always looked fresh, leaving their heads almost raw, with the bumps showing on their skulls.

She stopped to let them go past. None of them looked at her and the two men that walked last of all (rolled mackintoshes tight under their arms, hat-brims straightened in front) did not allow them to speak. The worn-looking leather football was carried, but not dropped or bounced or passed or tossed in the air, by the small black boy in front. Swinging their arms to keep warm, they headed back to the Mrs Moffet Home in Townsend Street.

In the field where the orphans played once a week, Margaret spoke to one of them, who had been sent to find the groundsman. "Are you really an orphan?"

"Aye," he answered with a Northern accent.

"Does that mean all of your family are dead?"

"I've brothers in two different homes: one in the Birds' Nest and one in Belfast. They never put us all together."

The whistle of the master interrupted them.

Just at the moment that William's hand got pinched in the chain of his trike, he and Margaret heard a familiar sound. Mrs Moore was coming along Tritonville Road, pushing her fish basket. The little front wheel squeaked, the left back one bumped and dragged. Every Friday and fast day she sold fish everywhere between Ringsend and Merrion Road.

As Mrs Moore bent over William, turning the pedals to free his fingers, quietening his distress, Margaret was thinking that she had never seen her so close before. With her black eyes, strong nose and gold earrings, she had something of the gypsy about her. Like the board laid across the basket, the handle of her knife, the apron folded up into a pocket for the money, even her down-trodden shoes, Mrs Moore's hands were covered with scales. Margaret and William had squatted so long in the tar-covered road that when they moved the crepe shoes of their sandals lifted strings of odorous squelchy tar.

Later that morning, Mrs Moore's fish round brought her to their house. Mama went out to thank her for her help. Mrs Moore declined to come in and have tea. She listened with her usual gravity, her high mouth, full of long teeth, smiling only briefly. As she talked, she continued to reach deep into her basket, laying a fish on the board, and slicing it up with a short knife, its handle bound with cord. Then she wrapped the herrings, the mackerel, now shorn of their heads and tails, squared off, in a sheet of off-white paper.

Only in Findlater's could you buy the packets of chocolate finger biscuits — bound, like a bundle of sticks, with a narrow band of paper around the foil. When Mama went to give her weekly order she usually brought the children. Overhead a little container stuffed with money shot rapidly along the wire, obeying the jerk of a straight handle pulled by the assistant. It reached the glass-fronted office high up at the end of the shop. Here all the wires ended and girls in dark blue overalls controlled the traffic and stuck papers onto a spike. In front of the fruit counter there sometimes stood a dumpy sack of walnuts.

After the long wait in the queue their turn had come to move, one by one, to Santa's side where he put his arm around them and (looking closely out of blue eyes) spoke from a white beard that made his lips seem pink and soft.

Amid the noise and the anxious crowds Margaret felt beguiled, charmed by his goodness. Now that she had spoken to him, this year she would surely get the lead farm set: animals, farmer with gun and dog, farmer's wife with basket and hen food.

This Santa, in Pims', was the last and finest of those they visited. Seeing him just before Christmas wiped out some of the bad things like the ignoble woman Santa, betrayed by her long crimson nails, like a witch.

The sills, the roofs, the trees, were wadded with snow. A soft feather now and then floated free from one part of the mass to another. From Dutch's arms Margaret shifted around to see the whole night. The snow, which Dutch had lifted her from bed to see, was less astonishing than the way hard specks of stars glinted in an enamel blue sky.

Next morning, she almost expected the snow to be still a lustrous blue wadding, when by then sills, roofs and trees looked ruined, not finished off, ragged, not cushiony.

When Margaret or William had a cough, Mama, and more rarely Dada, rubbed Vick on their chests. From the jar, jewel blue, came trailing lumps of the sharp-smelling stuff. Even to see a lump on Mama's fingertips started wild giggles, deep chuckles, plunging and thrashing around. Mama moved very fast to get in under their guards and scoop large fingerfulls onto their squirming bodies. But Dada would tap a small amount of Vick neatly on their skin and rub it in, before moving to the next section.

Even though it was late and dark when the family came out of the Queen's Theatre and crossed the road at the spot under the railway bridge, Margaret for once did not fear the window of the monumental sculptors. She had always felt cold when she looked in at the tombstones (some shiny black, some perfect white, and some the colour of reddish brawn) and at the blanched eyeless statues. But tonight she was trying to fix in her mind the way the pantomime boy had been: this year Robin Hood, last year Aladdin, always Gloria Greene striding, smiling, singing in a glow of mastery over villains and goodies alike.

[13]

Dada was changing his job. He left the newspaper to become the editor of a new, smart magazine. His colleagues had gifts engraved with his initials: P.H., for Patrick Hogan: a gold Parker pen and ballpoint in a rectangular box, a Ronson lighter in a stitched felt case and, most splendid of all, a cigarette case inside the lid of which the scratched silver scrawl of their signatures could be seen but not, by the children anyway, deciphered. Across the case was stretched an elasticated silk-covered band, like those that men wore on the sleeves of their shirts. Later it became frayed and slack because Margaret and William were always snapping it whenever they found the case in Dada's bedside locker. He left it and the lighter at home mostly, and after a while the little screw from the bottom of the lighter got lost. Margaret had loved watching him fill the lighter with petrol from a yellow plastic case shaped like a torpedo, the end of which he snipped off with a penknife. He kept his penknife in a small pocket of his jacket, but even into this one the tiny yellow shreds that gave all his clothes the smell of tobacco — the man's smell Margaret loved — found their way. Later she noticed sweets (mints, mostly, in twisted blue and white wrappers) more and more in his pockets.

Sometimes they were allowed to lie in their parents' big bed and watch Mama and Dada dress to go out. Mama's wardrobe was much bigger than Dada's, and both were made of warm-looking wood with a pattern of smoke. He put on his black tie and evening suit, the lapels faced with shiny material, and Mama wore an elegant cream dinner dress. Going to bigger dos, he donned a suit they called penguin, with tails and two buttons at the back. The white tie he wore with this suit he assembled from little lengths of material. There were several kinds of stud, which had to be retrieved from the corners of Mama's drawers. They always smelt of face-powder. Her black dress reached to the floor and the sleeves were transparent; everything that went with the dress was black or white: the cameo brooch, the delicate cocktail watch.

Of the two routes into town, the Number 2 and Number 3 bus took the more interesting one. Coming out of Ringsend the road rose steeply, and on that bridge Margaret had seen the squares of workingmen marching to Mass for the dead Pope in their best belted overcoats of navy and brown nap. Just over the bridge, at the Irish Glass Bottle Company, she saw from the top of the bus heaps of cullet and imagined the glare of the furnaces, as once she had seen in a short at the cinema men's cheeks bulging with the effort of filling frail-looking bubbles of glass from their lungs. Stains of oil that never disappeared lay on the concrete apron of the huge bus garage opposite the greyhound track. At night, buses were packed away in neat rows.

The sooty glass and bricks of the Gas Company buildings dispersed over the whole area an economy of gas, a climate of gas almost. The air always stank faintly of gas and the grass in the small square was cindery. Everywhere, looming over the streets with their cheerful or dingy small houses, were the gasometers, the chimneys, the hills of coal, the beginnings of dockland with its cranes.

Before the point where town proper began and the streets became more ordinary, more respectable, the area opened into a dock at one side. Here coalships — from Liverpool perhaps — discharged and took on cargoes.

While Carmel and Joe, her husband, were waiting for their house in Drimnagh, they lived in a little flat in Pearse Square, where gaslights beside the mantelpiece still worked.

Joe was an actor in his spare time and Margaret and William went to see him play the part of Archbishop Doyle in a show at the Brothers' School. They passed under an arch where the word Infants could only barely be made out on the grimy brick. The play (by a Brother who taught Senior English) showed the Archbishop on trial and tortured by English judges. Iron shoes filled with fat were heated at the fire until the flesh fell off the bones of his feet. In one book of *Snow White* the same thing had happened to the wicked queen, but she had to dance in the shoes until she dropped. The effect of stoking the fire was done with lights and red paper. The boys' cheeks were pink and their eyes glittered as they enacted the parts of soldiers, priests and members of the bishop's flock.

"I think we all agree that Joe here showed a fine bearing as a holy and learned man," said the Brother who spoke at the end.

Margaret and William were brought to visit Carmel's new house, the garden full of bricks and builders' rubbish, the new shiny wardrobes and the suite of red-upholstered furniture. Carmel's coat was loose, and she looked very big under it.

At home, Margaret asked Dutch about Carmel, "Why is she so fat?"

"She isn't fat, it's just her coat."

"But she looked just the same without her coat," protested Margaret.

When Mama's father died, she appeared with a black dress and stockings, thin seams down the backs of her legs. She also seemed fat, but Margaret did not say anything about it. She heard Dutch on the phone saying that Mama should not go to her father's funeral because of the baby. What was she talking about?

One day Mama was gone and when Margaret was standing in front of the big round mirror of her dressing-table, so strange without her things all over it, Dutch came in and said that they had a new little sister now.

When they climbed onto her bed, it was Mama herself that seemed new: bright-eyed, with her hair tied back and a bed-jacket trimmed with ribbons. On the table lay a cream and brown box of chocolates with Mary — the chosen name — written on it. They peeped at the baby's creased scarlet face, her curled hands. Margaret was angry that Mama was staying in hospital with Mary while they went home, and later, that she was allowed to sleep in Dada's and Mama's room. Even her attempt to make use of the new arrival at school misfired.

"Sorry I'm late Miss Dillon. We've just got a new baby sister."

Miss Dillon spoke in an audible aside to another teacher. "It's all a story. They'd say anything."

Desperately, Margaret insisted that she truly had a new sister. When he arrived to collect them, Dada confirmed her story, but she didn't feel it really counted or that she wanted to rely on Miss Dillon ever again.

Eating the laburnum seeds was very little fun, but everyone went through with it rather than be the first to leave. The shrivelled black things like small peas stood out later, unchanged, here and there through the frothy, lemon-coloured vomit.

Dr. O'Beirne's surgery was behind a chemist's shop. On dark shelves stood tall bottles with glass minarets for stoppers, their huge sides bellying, bulging, enclosing liquid of blue and red that would certainly taste sweet. For what sickness would they be prescribed?

The chair carried an advertisement for Gardenia perfume. A single long-stemmed red flower stood out on its black curvy back. Margaret thought at once of Mama. She was glamorous, like the name and smell of the perfume, the shape and materials of the chair. She was as different from other people's mothers as it was from the dining or kitchen chairs they sat on at home. Mama should have stood one of those Coty chairs in front of her dressing table where she kept her silver manicure case, her brushes and hand-mirrors, her hairpins and eyebrow tweezers.

The little box-shaped drawers at the chemist's had labels with difficult names: Attar of Roses, Valerian, Camphor, Oleum Coriandri, Eucalypti, Juniperi, Tinctura Myrrhae. They seemed holy, these names. They gave a hint of broken fragrant things, of the Wise Men's gifts, of pastes of dried flowers, of the oils sealed in a tiny silver box that the priest had used at Mary's christening.

In the surgery Margaret stood across the table from a portly stern man whose ponderous cheeks were of an ashy mauve colour.

"Well, what has she been up to — eating too many sweets?" he asked.

"No, laburnum seeds," Dutch said.

"We'll have to send the lady with the pumps, so, won't we?" he laughed with bogus joviality.

The lady with the pumps lived in Ringsend, in a small street near the pawnbrokers. In response to a message left with her niece, she came the next day. The things she brought in a serviceable leather bag were frightful: tubes and hoses, which she filled from a basin of soapy water with a rubber bulb. After seemingly harmless squelching came an awful urge to let everything out, so strong and so sudden that Margaret could hardly last as far as the toilet; and afterwards she sat shivering: emptied, weak and sticky.

"Has she used the child's chamber yet?"

Margaret had wondered what the strange word on the large box meant, the day Mama had brought it home from town. She was let down when a pot, made of dull pink plastic, was revealed. The name had become a joke.

Bus journeys without adults, like on the Number 18 home from school, were quite different from the trips into town. The school bus-stop was beside a factory where blind people made basketwork. In their old-fashioned suits they came out for lunch and stood, turning their heads to listen for approaching buses. Most of them got on to the Number 10, like the old woman. How unlucky to be blind and not be able to keep away from her! Her legs, as devoid of shape as if they had been twigs, were covered by wrinkled stockings, marked by stains of what had dripped and trickled from between her legs.

Though the Number 10 looked more interesting, in the very emptiness of the 18 lay its advantage. By the time it had reached the terminus, the top deck was usually deserted and (if Margaret and William disobeyed orders and went that far) they could hang onto the bar as it lurched around the corner and, for a brief moment, feel themselves to be Captain Carlsen aboard his listing ship out in the Atlantic. The motion of the bus had to serve as the swell of the huge sea, their gaberdines as his jacket with the brass buttons, the geometry sets in their schoolbags as the instruments with which he checked the angle of incline.

In the dark, even after the back of the door had lost its fearful quality, some charm was still needed. To run through the names Margaret heard some times on the BBC — Viking, Cromarty, Forties, German Bight, Fastnet, Finisterre — made her feel like one who, in an *Arabian Nights* story, had turned the peg on the neck of the wooden horse and gone whirling through the dark sky. Dutch wouldn't have been pleased about her way of sleeping or where she kept the hot-water bottle, so if anyone came in Margaret would roll it quickly to the end of the bed and cross her hands over her chest as Dutch had instructed the children to do. But they had seen her asleep and knew that she herself didn't.

As they came near the RDS the barking and yapping grew louder, the different tones forming a dissonance, dying away and reviving, as if some starting signal had instantly activated the chorus. Margaret and William walked through rows of boxes on top of which were little pens. Here owners as varied as their dogs combed and comforted Kerry Blues, Staffordshire Bull Terriers, Pekes and Samoyeds. Dog breeds had been a hobby of Margaret's ever since they had had a pedigree dog in the family — poor Flash had suffered from fits and had been given away. She longed to stay and learn, to hear about the dogs' character, diet and regimen. But with Dada little time was spent on the actual dogs. They always headed for large yards, one side of which accommodated a bar where men stood ten deep. After what seemed ages, he came back with a small golden drink for himself and two large reddish ones for them. They would always have theirs finished first, despite the difference in size, and would start pulling at his arm for more lemonade, for permission to go off back to the dogs, for a sign of recognition of their presence.

But he was always caught up with cronies from the newspapers or the radio station, writers, army officers, who put their hands on the children's heads, ordered them more drinks and settled into chat. Dada was always just about to move, he said, but they turned in boredom to picking up cigarette packets from the churned-up, mud-smeared grass until, as the dogs' cries continued, the crowds (shamrock now somewhat shrivelled on their coats) began slowly to move off towards the buses creeping along the Merrion Road past the queues ruffled by the mean March wind.

Margaret didn't like having her picture taken with Cormac, as he had growled at her once and no-one else had heard. But his army officer owner was a friend of Dada's and he always bought them orange, so she tried to ignore Cormac's lean restless body, the steaming tongue that lolled over his teeth, and the red teat-like shape that came out of his mickey, appearing surprisingly, from a hole that looked as if it had been made with a pin.

They didn't need a bus, of course; they lived so near and as they got older Dada often brought them across the road, leaving them to go home by themselves, while he headed for the Red Bank with people he had met at the Dog Show. That was a kind of culmination to the let-downs of the day.

As a bachelor, Dada had spent long periods on holiday in a hut he owned with some friends. It stood in a field under a hill where a lone chimney was the last remaining evidence of a leadmine, now totally worked out. His unmarried friends, Jim and Noel, continued to go there, and one August Saturday he brought the family for a day. He found again the haphazard masculine style of housekeeping he liked; the strong tea brewed until it was acrid, the greyish slices cut from large loaves, the butter eaten straight from the packet. Jim's father, now in his eighties, sucked something he had spooned up from a cup. Margaret leaned over to see what it was: bread soaked in milk.

"It's because he has no teeth," Mama explained.

In the afternoon they set out to walk to the beach. The big hearty man, Jim, who was her father's oldest friend, parted his hair almost in the middle of his head. His teeth were even, his nose straight, his cheeks washed with red.

"Onward, Christian soldiers," he chuckled when, their walk hardly begun, the rain started and wet grass and brambles stuck to their legs.

By the time they reached the sea, the mist was thick and everything was dim and muddled. After scrambling down a slope to a coarse shingle beach, they found nothing to do except return to the hut, now stuffy from the small paraffin heater. The toilet was alarming: a kind of board with a hole in it; and when Margaret looked down, she thought it must be a glimpse as far as the centre of the earth.

They stayed too late that evening, because Dada hated getting up to leave anywhere and always sought to soften, to postpone breaks. From the low door damp and darkness swallowed them up. Jim came with them across the field, as by then Mary had to be carried. The bus swept up to the stop in front of the pub, a box blazing with yellow light. They had to go upstairs, as both Dada and Mama smoked, and Margaret had the pleasure of sitting in the front seat, trying to pick out where they now were, at Monkstown or already at Blackrock, as drops trickled through the patches of steam on the windows and the baby slept, her forehead flushed, her mouth open.

Like the summer (threatened by the chill air and by the small patches of brown spotting odd trees) a phase in the occupancy of the hut was ending. Departures and re-orderings were marking the course of time. Jim was going to marry the girl who had also been visiting there. Once he settled down in a bungalow he would come only for occasional weekends to the hut. Sometimes the old man would be brought down. Noel would attempt to carry on the pattern of their former lives, going to dances in Woodbrook Golf Club, or in hotels in Bray, spending Christmasses at the houses of married friends whose growing children would wonder more with each elapsing year why he came, since they barely knew him.

Just before the curtain went up at the Gaiety matinee there was a moment of dizziness, of excitement, that could hardly be contained. Then, without a sound, the curtain rose on an empty stage. As if wafted by the music, by the smell of hot lights and greasepaint, a woman dancer appeared. Her scraped-back hair was like a doll's, her dress stiff and frilly, the stocking that covered her strong calves and thighs a dull white. When they touched the stage, her pink satin shoes made a knocking sound. They had blocks inside them, Margaret knew. She had already felt inside a pair, though her own studies in ballet had not reached the level of dancing in them. Cotton wool was put over the block so that it wouldn't hurt, but even so the thought of bearing down with her weight on the blocks made Margaret shiver. She could not separate it from the terrible story of the girl whose feet would not stop dancing, even when they were cut off by a train. From her seat in the dress circle stalls (the nicest of all in the theatre) she could make out the dancer's set face, whipping around like a fairground figure as she carried off a series of *fouettés* and then pirouetted across the stage. When she stopped, her shoulders continued to rise and fall faintly and her arms and legs were tense.

Then the music became more urgent, and a man burst on to the stage. He wore a velvet tunic that ended at the waist and a pair of white tights, with a prodigious bulge in front that Margaret kept looking at, though it seemed to her as if no one else had noticed. His shoulders and chest were well-developed, so that he seemed top-heavy as he sprang on small feet in apparently ribbonless shoes. He danced alone at first, leaping into the air in the step called *entrechat*, which brought him down with a different foot in front each time. Then he joined the woman and she pirouetted with his hands on her waist and fell to each side in turn, supported by his arms. When she thought about being so close to a man like that, Margaret always resolved to practise her own ballet steps more diligently. In the books she read, girls who kept on working at ballet (often in cold rooms and under the direction of ferociously stern teachers) were spotted by important people like Dame Ninette de Valois or Anton Dolin. In spite of their names, both of these were Irish by birth, and that sounded like a lucky omen, she thought.

Some day she might be one of the novitiate, her hair secured with a band — blue or pink, according to grade, the same colour in a sash on her black leotard — working through the boring drill that alone could release the grace, the energy of her body.

The interval was spent in the tea-rooms. The chairs were low, basketwork painted silver. Homely waitresses brought homely cakes, tea and extra hot water in silver pots that were pitted with frequent wear. They seemed as a consequence more seasoned, better wrought, than the newer, less flawed teapots of the Capital or the Monument Creameries. Margaret mixed and mashed her icecream with a flat wooden spoon, till the last part became runny, half-melted with the heat of her hand on the waxed paper. People she hadn't noticed at the ballet itself came over and talked. They made jokes she didn't understand, leaning back, sipping at tea and cigarettes. An American film director with a long horsey face, a growling voice and loose fawn clothes introduced his new very young wife.

Margaret liked the made-up actor best. He wore a black suit and a white shirt without a tie. His hair and eyes were a rich brown, his voice full of thrilling notes as he leaned forward towards Margaret, to shake her hand. Every move he made was full of grace, as he gathered one hand under his chin, the fingers curled, or patted the back of his hair while he talked.

"Ah yes, but Alexandria was frightful, my dear."

"Do tell about it," urged a woman in a fur coat.

"Well, flies, don't you know, simply swarming, and we all caught the virulent (he drew the word out) local form of Mediterranean tummy. All except Peter. He took care of us all beautifully."

When the ballet ended, Margaret was swept up by the combined impressions of scenery that bulged and rippled here and there without losing any of its magic suggestiveness, of smiles and hands lifted to stem the applause but only making it swell, of a bar across the middle of the exit door that gave way quite suddenly and thrust her back into the everyday world. It was almost a shock to discover that King Street was still there, with newsboys on the corner and crowds hurrying home up Grafton Street.

At school the next day, Margaret mentioned the actor she had met. Some of the girls had never heard of him, but Miss O'Rourke took a strong and unexpected interest in the matter. She told them all that he and another actor who worked with him were evil men. Refusing to say why, she left them wondering. It didn't seem to fit in with the subjects that were always troublesome, like having and feeding babies, the middle of the Hail Mary, or the first page of *Black Beauty*.

More than anything else, Margaret longed for a torch. It was partly because of what it would make possible — reading late at night under the bedclothes, and vaguer projects like exploring old houses, caves and secret passages. Itself an object of prestige, it made one important, the one who went ahead.

She had picked one out in the window of the new electrical shop beside Sandymount Green. It was the smallest of the range of black and silver torches that had, beside the on-off button, a little red one that enabled you to flash, at any speed required. She dreamed of signalling from the bathroom window to others out robbing orchards or tearing around the lanes. She would become the one to anticipate danger, detection or the intrusion of adults.

It took ages to reach the figure of 9/6d for the torch. But hiding away five shillings, in a new place, suddenly brought the whole scheme nearer to realisation. She handed over the coins and jubilantly received the torch, with two batteries that were held in place by a spring fixed under the cap.

She didn't, to be sure, make much use of the thing. There were certainly no occasions to warn or inform orchard-raiders or besiegers of the territory of adults. That sort of escapade was actually quite rare, depending on the presence of boys and on the humour they were in. Football had assumed pre-eminence among the sports they practised.

The reading under the bedclothes worked rather better, but the torch gave her heart-breakingly little value. Its tiny bulb grew dim, throwing a veiled light, and she changed the batteries around to no avail. Then she left it alone for a few weeks till the day when, newly equipped with money to buy batteries, she brought it back to the shop. But when the assistant opened the cap he could not extract the batteries. They had burst, filling the inside of the case with damp grainy white powder that defied any attempts to budge them.

"There's nothing I can do," he told her, giving back the useless, the hateful object. The disappointment making her reckless, mistrustful of the caution she felt had served her ill, she spent all the money for new batteries on bars of Bournville. Once she had crammed her mouth full and the sharp sweetness was coating her teeth, she felt a need to do something about the torch, which had so quickly become infuriating, a thing of mute reproach. With cold deliberation, she tossed it high into the chestnut trees, just inside Judge Shannon's big front gates.

She had often tried to dislodge conkers by throwing sticks and stones among those branches. Never before had she succeeded so well as this time with the torch. The bright green prickly cases that held startlingly new deep brown nuts — as if French-polished to a wondrous sheen — fell with muffled plops on the leaf-loaded drive. Then, remembering — and choosing to ignore — the use others could make of such a crop of conkers (William for schoolyard weapons, Mary for clumsy necklaces) she purposely broke into a run, sped on by her indifference, flat out, as fast as if the old judge in his long grey wig were chasing her.

Dada sometimes took days off, to bring Margaret and William in the later part of the morning into town. In the newspaper office, machines, some parts bright with oil, rattled and thundered, seeming to devour the trays of type that were being prepared on huge tables. Another day, they went to the radio station, above the GPO. A small man with a red face and husky voice conducted them along a cream and brown painted corridor as he talked to Dada. They saw a room full of strange things: a door with locks, bolts, bobbins, and latches of all kinds, fixed upright in a frame and leading nowhere; trays of gravel, pebble, tarmacadam and stone. There were, too, coconut halves to make the sound of horses' hooves. The man who worked all this magic wore a sleeveless pullover and smoked a lot.

For a long time Dada had been promising to bring them for a trip somewhere quite far, and one day he said they were taking the Enterprise from Amiens Street station to Belfast, where he had some business. Seen from the train, the city seemed already a new place: first, back gardens with washing; then later, a strange moment when there were mudflats on each side of the track, with a colourless sea beyond.

Dada had been joking with them about King Bully, as he called him, putting on a Northern accent. When they saw the mountains of Mourne, he sang them the Percy French song. That was when they were in the dining-room with the silver toast racks, the linen napkins and the sugar in little cubes.

In Belfast the policemen had revolvers on their belts and green uniforms, and a Union Jack flew over the City Hall in Donegal Square, though there Donegal didn't even sound the same as at home.

"I never saw men with guns before."

"You saw them at the Military Tattoo, Margaret, when you were very small."

"What was that? Did I not go too?"

"You stayed with Carmel, William. Do you remember, Margaret, begging to go back and look at the figure hanging from a parachute? I bet you've forgotten all about it."

Without asking, Margaret knew that it had been at the RDS, the roped enclosure, beyond which had hung the dummy.

Because of Braggarty (William's private name for the King of England) they took care not to be too impressed by the big hotel on Victoria Avenue, or the shops which, in truth, were less smart than those in Grafton Street. But to go asleep in a room overlooking buses and neon signs was exciting.

At the top of a drive, a figure with an upraised arm (they heard his name was Carson but felt no wiser) summoned them towards a stone building set in empty, perfectly tended grounds.

Just before they left for home on the train, pockets full of Spangles and Mars Bars that couldn't be had in the South, Dada bought them orange in a pub opposite the station.

"You've seen this place, in 'Odd Man Out'," he told them, and they remembered Shell meeting Johnny McQueen in a stall full of engraved glass and ornamental mirrors. The fugitive gunman and the city that had threatened yet sheltered him often featured in their games since Dada had brought them to that picture.

"The wee one has bitten off her glass," the barman told Dada when he came back from the toilet. Margaret was crying. She had felt the thin hardness come away and the cracks spread. The barman used a greyish cloth to carry the upsetting pieces and the pool of spilled orange to the edge of the table. He swept them into the ruined shaft of the glass. A few seconds later, everything was suddenly fresh again for Margaret. She drank another orange as Dada sat holding his cigarette cupped, smoke darkening the brown on his fingers.

That was what Johnny McQueen had done. Margaret thought of the face suddenly half lit-up as the man, alone and in hiding, drags greedily on a cigarette. She knew for a certainty that Dada had once done the same.

On the way to Herbert Park they always bought fishing nets in the tiny shop near the arch. A shrunken little lady (did she ever sit down, or was she afraid that then her view would be cut off?) handed the bamboo rods over the counter piled with Fry's Chocolate Cream and flanked with pinned up copies of the *Daily Mail*.

The little nets always got misshapen and came off the wire rings at the first few tries, so that they were too gammy to survive one day's outing. But the pond was probably thick with fish, because even the most incompetent angler always ended up with a few pinkeens. In the narrow confines of a jam-jar, held at eye-level, the huge greenish eye would look wobbly and scary like that of a sea monster, or the people who wore dispensary glasses with thick lenses. Though the kids always hopefully threw a bit of pondweed on the surface of the jarful, the fish were nearly all dead by the time they reached home: putting water and weed in a jam-jar did not make it like the pond nor undo the ravages they had so casually inflicted.

Near the pond, the rockery held greyish spiky plants, crystalline like the chunks of granite laid between them. Beside the fountain hung an iron cup on a chain. To drink from it was to taste stone and water and metal all at once. It was a frontier between the different kingdoms of nature as was the coppery seaweedy green of the stain on the bath at Killiney, or the plant-like fronds of the jelly-fish's tentacles.

On days when it had rained scents came up from the borders: the earth freshly plumped and pungent with the manure and crumbly peatmoss that the park-gardeners spread around the roots of flowers and shrubs.

Margaret, William and their friends liked best another, grimmer end of the park. Around by a huge log, stranded since some long-distant winter storm, stood the men's toilets. They had been told it was not safe to go too near that place. Strange men might be hanging around. As it was not explained why they were strange, or how you would know them, Margaret formed a picture of the kind of person to beware of. He did not look like the old man with the sack who went past the cottage in Killiney and according to Carmel was the bogeyman but, rather, like a man who was brought every Sunday to half-eleven Mass by his old parents. He gurgled a lot, and his hair looked like the soft prickles of a baby hedgehog. As his parents grew thinner and wearier, he seemed unchanged: still round, still wetly pink, his hands smooth and soft, pulling at their sleeves to let him look at the candles on the side altars after Mass.

The log was ugly, like a great sightless whale. It was

stripped of most of its bark, scored with penknifed traces of names, and it could not be imagined growing upright, in leaf or in blossom. When they were younger it had been boat, horse, car, sledge or dolls' bed. Now it was a wall to be scaled by attacking forces, held by occupiers, an obstacle to be vaulted over, the focal point for treks and hunts, the home or den of all their games, itself virtually immovable, except for occasional concerted attempts to investigate the pullulating life of woodlice and earthworms it concealed.

The dark picture in oils over the classroom fireplace showed Jesus sitting among the doctors in the temple. The girls knelt behind their desks for morning prayers, varied only in so far as they were followed by a different hymn for each month. As the sound trailed away, desk lids were banged, chairs grated on the floorboards. Since the tiny fireplace in that classroom gave so little heat, was so often blocked off by the teacher standing in front of it, Margaret tried to secure a place near the window. The road, though far away, could be clearly seen, and the old man from next door, who went out to Searson's on the dot of 11.15 each day, would herald the break.

After break they had History with Miss McCarthy, who had come just that year. Her dark brown eyes were very small, her nose flat, and her little body continually nervous. She wore high heels, the peeptoes adorned with bows. They noticed her shoes because one day, in a vain effort to keep order, she had stamped so hard that the heel had come right off. The class had broken up in pandemonium, and from then on Miss McCarthy's accounts of the grievances of the Irish people at English hands found even less response than before.

Yet, though it would never have done to say so, Margaret, for one, was gripped by Miss McCarthy's fiery and partisan teaching of history, at least of recent history. Her stories about people with green-stained mouths, the chewed grass dripping as they collapsed in their cabins or along the roads to the ports for America, or about those who had taken soup during the Penal Days and whom the justice of God had punished on their deathbeds when the soup leaked from their bodies, did not quicken as did her accounts of the Easter sacrifice of 1916. Margaret read and re-read the last chapter in the history book and the articles in the Capuchin annual (on her father's bookshelf) where Father Aloysius had recorded his memories of attending the prisoners in Kilmainham and Arbour Hill at their executions.

For a time, the only items in the museum that appealed to her were the cases holding slouch hats, drab green tunics, ammunition cases and holsters, the leather now cold and stiff to the eye. The men who had worn these seemed to her real, though exalted, nearly like saints. Their photos, the reminiscences of their mothers and sisters, testified to a purity which was manly, innocent, high-hearted. As they seemed to her to have been more alive, so did they now seem more dead than the skeleton found in a bog, which might as well have been a long sod of turf.

She struggled to put into words her feelings about Ireland, England and their unhappy past, to make of them poems that would be as good as the one she learned in school, called 'I remember', especially the bit about the poet wishing that he had died during his childhood: "But now I often wish the night had borne my breath away."

She wouldn't go in. It would be easy to say that she had missed the bus back, then thought it was too late. She was free, without so much as a schoolbag, till Mooney's clock on the bridge showed her it was time to go home. Once the decision was made, the whole thing was easy. But once the decision was made, others had to follow. What to do? Where to go? She lacked both money and nerve to go further than Baggot Street. Excursions, after all, required planning. But all the Baggot Street shop windows were there to be, for once, savoured at leisure.

The Monument Creameries: a hunk of butter on a sort of platform made of white china; trays of eggs: white, brown, warmly speckled and a smaller number of magically-coloured duck eggs. On the black and white tiles stood rows of tilted glass-fronted biscuit tins. Everything was as clean as the sheets of waxy paper they wrapped around irregular bricks of butter.

In Lipton's, neat stacks of various kinds of rasher from the fine pearly back to the raggedy darker coloured collar rashers and the streaky, with a little core of gristle in each one.

Across the bridge to Parsons: Hans Anderson and Oscar Wilde's *Tales* in the window. A waft of chemical from the cleaners', where boys and girls could be seen opening and closing a huge press, leaving behind each time a pair of trousers or a raincoat, flattened out and penetrated with steam. In Creamer's, bowls of sweets lined with doilys stood on little pillars, but she had no money to spend.

A feeling of boredom led her to consider the condition of her classmates and, passing near the corner, she looked up at the school windows as if she could descry them occupied in analysis of sentences and parsing. The weariness of mid-afternoon would already have invaded the classroom. She was really lucky to be out in the air, free, in the promise, the wide expanse, of Pembroke Road. But houses and gardens that seemed so intriguing when she had time only to pass quickly by offered little diversion now, so that she found herself facing Mooney's clock for the third time, and the hands still stood at ten to three. Had the thing stopped?

Even the street, innocently busy as it had seemed at first, was taking on a different air. It was dumb to have gone mitching without a companion, without provision of money or sweets, above all, without venturing some distance from the school. She could be recognised, questioned, at any moment. She began to fancy that everyone would guess she had no proper reason for being out. She might even see someone from school on a message to buy pants for a young child who had had an accident.

She felt a certain relief in heading for the side door, intending to show up for the end of the English class. But once set the course of events proved difficult to alter. The side door was locked. To go in by the front would have attracted too much attention. She had to go home with a story that they had all been let out early.

The next day Miss Dillon was stern. Margaret's story that she had missed one bus at lunchtime and found the door locked when she returned — as it happened, only partly untrue — she discounted totally.

"I know from the black spot on your tooth."

By the time Margaret reached home to look in the mirror, the spot had, apparently, disappeared.

The summer holidays and the month they spent in Killiney were always alike, differing chiefly in whether more picnics were eaten at the rented cottage (after a kind of retreat from the rain) than on the hill or the beach; whether they suffered from sunburn blisters or from colds; whether they brought a cat, or a dog, or both, or neither; whether in the course of the month friends came down, necessitating complicated juggling of beds and blankets.

But Killiney in the summer was a series of constants: like the hill that plunged steeply downwards so that descent to the beach was unavoidably a precipitation, ascent back to the cottage as unavoidably a laborious trudge. It seemed that they had always had permission to go alone to the shop, directly opposite the cottage, where the step was much higher on one side than on the other because of the slope of the hilly street. It seemed that they had always reached the beach after a pell-mell rush through dark lanes scented with the nuts of eucalyptus trees that overhung the rough stone walls.

It seemed that ages of still, endless hours of daylight had gone by while Margaret stood at the low wall, opening up tightly shut buds of veronica that overlapped, getting smaller as they moved through a range of greens, from dark to paler, to greyish, to a point where they were mauve and the flower (sealed in the inmost, tiniest sheath, from which it would never now emerge) was revealed.

Snaps entrapped single incidents, salient because so re-corded: Mama gone half-way down the hill before she realised she was still wearing her plaid bedroom slippers, William catching a stubby dogfish, Mary holding up a bar of chocolate that had actually melted with the heat, Carmel shooing them in from the garden at bedtime to escape the bogeyman, Dada holding Margaret on a donkey's back, Dutch testing the temperature of the water with her toe.

Like assays, the snaps revealed variations in height, in hair-cuts, in numbers of teeth, of freckles, at different times. But they sampled a substance that was fused, compounded into oneness.

One sweltering day Margaret remembered without the aid of any snaps. The three of them — Mary was by then big enough to come along — decided on Whiterock, instead of Killiney, beach and the dog, Caesar, was particularly giddy that day. Near the beach he was distracted by the sight of cats, which he felt obliged to pursue down a long leafy drive. By the time they had burst out onto the brightness of the beach, Caesar had caught up on them. His tail was drooping and he was accompanied by a tall boy wearing a wristwatch.

"Is this idiotic dog yours?" he asked. "My aunt's cats soon dealt with him. Next time, keep him out of her garden."

Automatically, they sought to even the score.

"We couldn't care less about going into your aunt's stupid garden, anyway," rejoined William.

"This looks like a boring place, with so many little kids," the newcomer went on, with a glance at Mary, who was already intently pulling off her clothes, thinking, that with the older ones so engrossed, she might for once be the first to hit the water.

"I suppose you lot swim off the beach, that's kids' stuff. I'm going to dive."

He raced towards a line of rocks that stuck out into the sea, then took his time and moved circumspectly over them. Turning back to make sure that they were all watching him from where they were bobbing near the beginning of the deep part he undressed to the togs he was wearing under his clothes.

He went through a lot of business, removing his watch ("I hope he drops it, the show-off," muttered William), yanking up his togs, raking back his hair, as if posing. When he actually broke the film of still water in the lee of the rock with a questing dive, he was giving more attention to the onlookers than to the sea. As they reached the spot, his face came up beside their feet, still grinning.

On the deep, shaded lee of the rock, ripples set up by his plunge were full of clusters of jelly-fish, swinging dreamily backwards and forwards.

He was out of the water before he began to feel the stings. By the time he had reached his aunt's house, the shirt he had pulled on over his togs was causing him so much pain that he could hardly keep from crying, despite his thirteen years. All rivalry forgotten, they went with him, carrying the rest of his stuff. William took particular care of the watch.

They also helped when, some days later, he returned to the beach and took revenge on the jelly-fish. He brought a large, businesslike landing net with a steel handle and fine green meshes, which belonged to his uncle. They held him by the legs while he leaned over the pool and scooped up numbers of the translucent creatures. Swinging in triumph the bag of nacreous clotted stuff he scattered squealing bunches of girls as he chased them along the beach.

Then he spilled the jelly-fish onto the hot stones and watched with satisfaction as they sank from free and active creatures to glutinous patches, then to wet stains, till they were no more.

"Come on, Margaret," shouted the tall boy from the iron steps by which he, William and Mary were making their way up to his aunt's house. As she joined them, Margaret had not quite forgotten about the jellyfish. She was thinking about their swimming beat, the strong contraction of their bells like the forcible closing of an umbrella, and of the way their milky mauve bodies could inflict pain with what felt like a caress.

That was, though they didn't know it then, the last

summer in Killiney.

II

THE GAME OF snap-apple was followed by a tea of sandwiches and brack. Then, comfortably supplied with bowls of nuts and sweets, the girls bunched around the fireplace to hear Cecilia's ghost story.

"There was this little maid, in a lonely old house, miles out in the country. Her mistress was a cripple and was very mean to her. Every time she got back to the kitchen the mistress would ring her bell again and call her back again, for no reason. The girl couldn't stand it any longer, and one day she smothered her with her pillow. She thought of selling the lovely rings the old lady wore, and tried to pull them off. But the fingers were swollen and she could not force them off. Desperate, she got a carving-knife, and cut fingers and all off. When knocking suddenly sounded through the large house, she panicked and put the fingers under her own pillow for safety.

The next day the stagecoach to London would pass the crossroads, and she would leave that horrible place for ever, to enjoy a life of comfort and become a lady. The evening was coming on by the time she got rid of the caller, who had turned out to be the steward. As she washed the last traces of blood from her hands at the big stone sink in the kitchen, one of the bells on the board over the pantry door jangled. Sick with fear, she noticed that it was her mistress' bell.

That night, in her little attic, she finally dropped into a restless sleep, but wakened to the creak of the door and the hiss of her mistress' voice.

'Why didn't you come when I rang? You've got something of mine . . . You've got something of mine under your pillow, and I've come to take it back . . . I'm inside the door . . . I'm crossing the room . . . I'm standing beside your bed . . . I'm feeling under your pillow . . . Wowh!" and Cecilia pounced forward, snapping the tension she had created. Before the punch line, a small girl had already raced to the lightswitch, and normality was restored with the brightness, as a burst of nervous laughter allowed them all to shrug off how tightly the story had gripped them.

A number of other girls also walked down Herbert Park on their way home from the party. As Margaret relished the delicious shiver of talking about ghosts under the dark line of poplars and later, as she went over the story in bed, she was probably already in love with Cecilia. But she didn't become fully aware of it until Cecilia winked at her, on the way to hockey on the Number 18 bus a few days later.

It was rare for anyone to join fourth year, so Cecilia's arrival made news. She was a big girl but she moved lightly. Her eyes shifted from blue through grey to green, she had long thick lashes and a strong chin.

In that class, talk about boys had been desultory. Though they were all going to their first mixed parties, where they rocked and rolled with brothers of friends or friends of brothers, and had vague episodes on holidays at Courtown or Lahinch, they kept discussion to small, tight groups. Cecilia gave a voice, and therefore a new outlet, to all these muted, submerged feelings. She had, she told her first acquaintance in the class (and the news spread quickly), a crush on the tympanist in the Radio Eireann Symphony Orchestra, a

[38]

swarthy German. She insisted on the word tympanist —
drummers were in showbands.

Within a week, the class was caught up in a fever of
schemes to get free (or at least cheap) tickets for concerts.
Cecilia was skilled at winkling out information about times of
rehearsal and (during the Dublin Grand Opera season) at
organising parties to go into town and queue in relays for the
gods. Except when a concert was given in Limerick or
Athlone, the orchestra rarely played anywhere that winter
without a contingent of Miss Dillon's girls, clapping enthusiastically.

Some of their number were detailed in advance to forego
their second round of applause so as to race down the innumerable steps of the gods and reach the stage door in time
to check discreetly which bus the young musician headed for.
They knew his name was Franz Muller.

With Cecilia's example so vividly before them, others of
the class declared their interest in other members of the
orchestra. Even from the front row of the gods, all the
younger men looked personable in their full dress suits. Carol
became attached to the French horn, while Suzanne and
Niamh hesitated between the bassoonist, the youngest
flautist, and the last violinist in the second row. It was a
major setback to discover the object of interest was married.
To find that the loved one was from, say, the North of
Ireland rather than Italy or Hungary, was also a blow, but a
lighter one.

As the youngest in the class, habitually quiet and reticent
about her life outside, even to her friends, Margaret might
have seemed an odd recruit to this band of enthusiasts. But
everywhere Cecilia made new configurations among existing
alliances. She had been put sitting beside Margaret the first
day, and she developed for her an affection possibly tinged
with curiosity about Margaret's status — partly but not
wholly willed — as a dark horse. Looking in with her during
the lesson on *As You Like It*, she found that Margaret had an
edition that included lines missing from other girls', and also
that she refrained from mentioning this fact to the teacher.

Cecilia did not confine herself to the notables of the class, but drew on diverse sources for support. There was also, inevitably, a practical advantage in being pally with Margaret. Once asked (and she had not been asked often before), Margaret was delighted to help, at least Cecilia, rapidly supplying answers to Latin, History or English questions. This helped compensate for the effects of nights spent out at concerts. Margaret attended the concerts only occasionally: she had no interest declared in any player and was, besides, taking schoolwork seriously that year. Cecilia had been left sitting beside her because if she were with one of the pals there would have been more talking. Cecilia took care to confide in her, so that the latest news of the concerts was at once known to her.

On hockey days, everyone went to the terminus of the Number 18 route. Cecilia sat on the long seat across the top, facing the other passengers. She happened to catch Margaret's eye and winked expertly, laughingly, with the perfect ease of a boy. Margaret was musing as she gathered her stick with the dangling hockey boots.

From then on, she was impatient with any tardiness from the younger kids she escorted to school. She arrived early in the morning, charged back immediately after lunch before the usual signal, the Swastika hooter, had sounded, and waited around at the end to see where Cecilia went afterwards. The last was important because, while Cecilia often led a giggling bunch of the pals on the Number 10, bound for Bewley's (where Franz had been spotted) or for the Gaiety booking office (where Cecilia had got pally with one of the clerks), more than once she had actually walked alone down Pembroke Road to the Number 8 bus-stop near the kiosk. And more than once Margaret had watched, chagrined, while she herself was carried past on a Number 18 surrounded by chattering 1st year girls. She (who would have walked much further than the kiosk — to Monkstown itself — in Cecilia's company) was powerless to do more than look back as long as she could still see the blue-coated figure.

In dreamy mood one afternoon, Cecilia seemed downcast

by the obstacles to meeting Franz before he got too friendly with one of the attractive lady musicians around. She suddenly felt, suddenly wondered at, Margaret's sympathy, her excitement. "I bet you've got someone you're keen on yourself, Margaret."

It was all moving very fast, suddenly, but Margaret couldn't forego the pleasure of admitting her love, even though she didn't dare elaborate. Thinking in terms of her own crush, Cecilia became even more cordial. When the teacher happened to be called away for a moment, she dug the shoulder of the girl in front.

"Hey, Niamh, Margaret has someone she likes, too. I might have guessed," she added enthusiastically. Margaret savoured her undivided attention. In the pause that followed, Niamh noticed that Margaret wasn't telling them any more, just sitting and smiling.

"You're right not to say much for the moment," whispered Cecilia as the teacher came back into the room.

"That's it," Margaret agreed.

In the weeks which followed, if she were late for school, especially happy or especially sad, falling behind or surging ahead in schoolwork, Cecilia interpreted it as caused by the unknown, unnamed beloved, the crush. It gave Margaret new prestige among the girls: she could murmur knowingly when they dwelt on the pains of love. She could imply that there were obstacles to her meeting him often. In the hints and shrugs, Margaret found precarious joy. The beloved acquired, perforce, some traits. When they asked, now and then, about him, she told them, now and then, about him — combining the red hair of one fellow with the long legs of another, with the teasing manner of a third. She fabricated a fair amalgam: he would have been fun, he would have been desirable, if he had existed, if she had loved him. It was true that she became almost fond of him in the end, before he finally sank back into the ghostly realm from which she had summoned him. But the charge of feeling with which she spoke of him to

Cecilia never attended him at any other time. It was not as the others thought: not a vague hope of seeing him, but the certainty of seeing her, that coloured and sweetened each day. For her, the obstacle was harder to surmount than time or place or adult opposition would have been. She invoked these because she was beginning to understand how much complications were regarded not merely as normal, but as enhancing to the whole business. She was also beginning to understand that none of the girls wanted to be surprised, to be overtaken by something totally new. Had she chosen, she would not have wanted it either, but by now there was nothing to be done. She was, then, at once reckless and circumspect; giving herself wildly to the feelings, but holding back from thinking too much about their meaning. That there was absolutely no-one that she could consider sharing them with was obvious. Such knowledge was at once a burden and her most valued prize.

No-one at home had ever known what she used to do in bed. Things like that were never mentioned, and at the school retreats the sessions that were popularly supposed to let the girls know all about sins against purity were short on definite facts. She knew only that if she were to confess these feelings the priest would tell her they were sinful. She did not want to hear that because she could not accept it, and she did not want to try and live without them.

Just sitting beside Cecilia, sharing Longman's *Latin Course* or Hall and Knight's *Algebra*, was at first richly satisfying, but as time went on it did not suffice. Never before had Margaret regretted so sharply the shortcomings of the school, the dearth of activities like plays or operas. Cecilia wanted to take up ballet, with Margaret, but the plans came to nothing: her mother had no time for pursuits of that kind.

That left only the hockey. At least during matches, a common purpose, a greater tingle in the atmosphere, marked a departure from routine.

Margaret found exhilaration in the tightening of her muscles, in the hard-drawn breath, the striving to score, of the bunch of players, red-faced, muddy-kneed, their breath hanging in the chill air. Alongside the pitch, somewhat on a higher level, an occasional train would pass, with a forlorn clang, through Sandymount Halt.

But the games were messy affairs, especially when (as frequently transpired) their opponents were also mediocre. Stoppages were frequent, when players had lifted their sticks too high, and Margaret felt the day run down quickly, to the moment when she turned in the direction opposite to Cecilia, towards tea and homework that, because of the hockey, would now take up much of the rest of the night.

One such evening, she was reading in her room a story — not the geography that had been set — when her mother called her to the phone. To her stunned elation, it was Cecilia.

"Margaret, I wasn't paying attention when she gave out the questions about Africa, and neither was Valerie or Carol. Can you tell me what they are?"

Margaret did not appreciate that chiefs have to keep all of their followers happy, that it was without malice that Cecilia shifted her favour. She could only think that if the Geography teacher had been better able to control the class, Cecilia would never have rung her.

"What's the matter? You sound a bit funny," said Cecilia when she had noted down the details.

"Nothing, I'm just surprised to hear from you. I didn't know you were on the phone."

"Gosh — did you not? We always have been, but Mummy's always on at me about running up a big bill. I'd better go and finish this Africa stuff. Thanks, Margaret. You're a star. See you tomorrow."

Margaret turned the pages of the directory till she found Cecilia's father's name. Just to read her address was good. But she kept thinking of her words. Cecilia often rang the pals and they rang her, about the crushes, and other matters too. What had given her the idea that Cecilia cared especially for her? She made use of her to keep abreast of work, that was all.

That night, in the darkness of their bedroom, Margaret

talked for two and a half hours about Cecilia to her sister. Mary was half asleep and answered only in grunts. Margaret had to talk about Cecilia: she had to say a great deal in order to conceal what she shrank from saying. So she went on and on till Mary was asleep, and after, about the musicians, the future plans (next time, to go up and ask for their autograph), even about Cecilia's first triumph with the ghost story.

As the 18 bus pulled around the corner, Margaret was prodding her young charges up the stairs. To sit on top seemed to signify more unconcern about the kiosk and who was walking that way.

By Easter Franz had left the RESO, and gone to the Leeds Philharmonic. Cecilia's visits to Bewley's had brought her and the pals into contact with boys from CUS. Before long, they were wearing blue and red scarves and going to rugby matches.

Cecilia left school after the Inter and took a secretarial course. One Sunday afternoon the following year Margaret ran into her on Dun Laoghaire pier. They were both with their mothers and the conversation was brief, except that Cecilia laughed at something Margaret said.

"I always thought you had the makings of a cynic." In their parlance, that was indeed praise.

Margaret pressed her ear to the frayed cloth of the front of the radio to browse around the stations of Europe, where a few inches on the dial would bring up first the American Forces' Network Gospel preaching, then what she recognised as being, sensationally, Communist propaganda. From a station in Czechoslovakia a woman read the news in metallic perfect English. She had a bun and a thin mouth, just as certainly as the American preacher had a crew cut and unflawed teeth. Margaret aimed always to come back to Radio Luxemburg in time for the Top Twenty, but not much before. Before the treacly voice announced that by his H. Samuel Everight Watch it was exactly eleven o'clock, she sometimes caught the homely tones of Horace Bottomley as he assured his listeners that they could win by using his

[44]

system of football pools. The records were played in the order of number twenty to number one. Margaret never missed the programme, at least not once during the year that began with the success of 'Rock around the Clock' and ended with that of 'What do you Want'.

Radio Eireann was another world, with symphony concerts, ceilis and Hospital Requests. To listen to the Walton's programme on Saturdays seemed a duty which for a time she ought not shirk. But the exhortation to sing an Irish song, even when backed up by ballads, rousing or comic, and fife and drum airs, could not long contend with Bill Haley, let alone Elvis.

One sponsored programme was tinged with more sophistication. It went out late at night and was presented by the Hospital Sweeps. As an institution, the Sweep was something like the programme: familiar, indubitably Irish, yet carrying a whiff of glamour, the glamour of big money and the racecourse, not mistrusted, not regarded as scandalous, rather somehow redeemed by the founder's national record, by his support (hence the title of the company) for the hospitals (many of them run by nuns), by his giving employment to widows and single women, among them Mama's friend, Marie.

At tennis, her partner ran after what Margaret liked to think were tricky, match-winning shots: punchy backhands and high lobbing forehands. Somehow, the games mistress looked more appealing in a white aertex blouse and short skirt than in what she called her "winter rig" of navy cardigan and gymslip. That an adult would actually choose to wear one of those despised garments, which they could not wait to lay aside, amazed the girls.

By the end of the lesson, the rubber of Margaret's racquet had discoloured her palm with a greyness that rubbed off in tiny rolls. Her mouth was hurting with a flat dryness, as she retrieved the last balls.

"Coming for a drink, you two?" shouted Niamh, from the next court. She swung back polished hair, donned sunglasses.

Margaret hated this moment. If it had been possible to

[45]

have a drink of water, without going into the clubhouse, she could have made a getaway. But the only tap was there, in the dusty room, shadowy after the sunlight, where drinks were served to those with money for them: measures of sticky cordial into the glass, then water to fill it up.

The girl with the sunglasses drank hers quickly, as she was going to have a second one. A sunbeam wobbled in the depths of the garnet or emerald liquid, slick on the sides of the glasses. Margaret never had two drinks: one was often a stroke of good fortune, made possible by the conductor having passed over her while collecting fares. If she had one, she made it last as long as possible: if she was having water, she drank it quickly. Neither drink was ever as cool or as pleasant as she anticipated. The shade of the clubhouse, that was really the good part.

Dutch kept a close eye on what the children heard and saw — vigilant to send Margaret out of the room when, in an O'Casey play on the radio, mention of an illegitimate baby loomed. Yet once she had cut out her puzzles — Spot the Ball and other competitions — from the *Sunday Express* (up to half a dozen copies, and as many of the *Dispatch* and *Reynolds News*) she left the papers there, unguarded, for anyone to read. In these papers there was question of much stranger and more disturbing matters than babies of any kind. In one photo a long queue of London housewives with shopping bags and toddlers by the hand wound around the garden of a small dismal house in Notting Hill. Detectives were busy digging up the remains, as they called them, of numerous women who had been murdered and buried there. The housewives stood patiently for hours in the hope of glimpsing a shoe, a bit of clothing, some part of a corpse. More and more photos appeared as the weeks went on: a man with horn-rimmed glasses and a long mackintosh, who was accused of the murders: his lodger, who had been hanged for murder some years before: and some of the victims. For the most part fuzzy, being enlargements of snaps taken automatically in Woolworths' cubicles, these carried reminders of long-gone hairstyles, neckscarves, eyebrows, lips. Many of them (including those with Irish names) had been prostitutes. Margaret didn't know what that word meant, but she understood it had something to do with London. The affair continued to fill the English papers, from the first discovery of a decomposing body to the reports of the execution. But the Irish Sunday papers, concentrating on accounts of Ireland's struggle for freedom and the secrets of Fatima, gave only brief mention.

The English King Braggarty whose profile was framed in a little oval above the scene of river or plain on stamps from Nyasaland and Tanganyika, whose faltering voice they listened to every Christmas afternoon, despite the ritual protestations of Dutch, died in his sleep one foggy night. At Miss Dillon's everyone wanted to rush home and hear his funeral described on the BBC. Sailors pulled the gun carriage with his body, and what survived of European royalty followed behind.

When his daughter, the Princess Elizabeth, was to be crowned Queen, the girls of Miss Dillon's were giddy and fascinated. They asked for time off to hear that broadcast too. During the day it floated tantalisingly from the flat overlooking the schoolyard. In this flat some students lived and, that day, they responded to the girls' signals to turn their radio up full and perch it on the window sill.

Miss McCarthy was indignant. "England is a pagan country — you shouldn't want to know anything about it." "But Miss McCarthy, the Queen is gorgeous, and we'll never get the chance again."

Despite her Republican leanings, Dutch brought Margaret and William to see a film of the Coronation. It was hard to fathom why, since in the discussions at meal-times she had unquestioningly sided with those (to judge from the letter columns, the majority) who thought that it should be refused a showing in Irish cinemas. Yet, hearing that a showing had been organised, she went with Margaret and William to a Baptist Hall in Exchequer Street. The music was loud, and because the projectionist had little experience in showing long films of the kind, it came in bursts from the ill-adjusted

[47]

sound equipment. The ceremony was archaic and slow-moving. Afterwards, most of the audience, transported with enthusiasm, stood up and applauded — not the organisers, the projectionist, or anyone actually there — but the images that had reassured, that had reminded them of the abiding presence of the monarchy.

Copies of the *Reader's Digest* often found their way into the house, as part of the bundles of magazines bought up at sales of work. Finally, Dutch started buying it regularly, after she had got a few copies as free samples in the post. The 'Condensed Book' section was usually unappealing to Margaret, dealing with loveable otters or philosophic old Middle West physicians. But noticing, one month, that it treated 'My Twenty Years in Soviet Prison Camps', she took the magazine to her room. There were sentences that she had to read over and over again, about the woman whose new baby had been taken from her and who had to squeeze the milk from her bursting breasts into a bucket, which was used in common by all prisoners in the hut. The guards, who were as brutal as animals, wore quilted coats and hats with ear-flaps, but the prisoners had only bits of rags tied even around their feet as they crossed the frozen ground of the compound.

Communists were mentioned very often in school, and not only in the Christian Doctrine class. Miss Dillon punished very bold conduct in the younger children by putting offenders behind the piano, there to kneel and pray for Russia.

One day, Miss O'Rourke showed them a picture of men in white uniforms and black caps in the act of shooting rifles at a statue of Our Lady that stood out amid the rubble of a half-ruined church. It seemed strange to waste bullets on a statue, but Miss O'Rourke explained, "These men hate God and they are fighting to make Spain Communist." The girls had never before heard of this war, in which Our Lady had assisted the army of General Franco so that Spain was saved for the Faith. The secrets of Fatima, which the Pope would reveal in the year 1960 ("only seven more years to go" exclaimed someone happily), would reveal to the Church and the world that Communists were trying to destroy all civilization. Only prayer could defeat them.

It was very hard to understand why the Communists were doing all this — removing people from their families and putting them into camps; and why things were so different in Ireland. "We have freedom to practise religion, to go to Mass and the sacraments, to learn Christian Doctrine."

Miss Dillon and the teachers were always very enthusiastic if anyone connected with the school happened to be mentioned in the papers. The brother of a girl in second year was one of four young men who sailed across the Atlantic in a yacht. To the girls' surprise and glee, the notice board in the hall (in their experience, hitherto rarely used) showed a newspaper cutting and photo of the crew. Three had huge dark beards, one a smaller lighter one, and all had bare chests. The hall — up to then quiet, except for illicit excursions on wet days to dispose of the scummy milk by pouring it into the rubber boots ranged along the wall — was populous with frisky girls, keenly comparing and appraising.

Hardly had they adjusted to the presence of the Jewish family, the Levys, on their quiet road, than Margaret's neighbours found further novelty in the news that the empty house — the one that had been to let for ages — had been taken by a family of foreigners, Norwegians: the Olsens.

On further acquaintance, they seemed more like two families than one, as if, in the hazards and confusions of the post-war years in their country, the urban, shady, bohemian mother and son on the one hand, had thrown in their lot with the rural, stolid father and daughter on the other.

Shortly before Christmas, the mother — Madame O as she always called herself — invited every child on the road to a party, even the Jews and the very wild boy with the Dublin accent. The disregard for the nuances of social intercourse suggested by this gesture was confirmed by the garb she chose for the occasion — considered odd for an elderly woman. They later realised that of course she never wore anything other than a thick sailor's jumper, corduroy trousers and tennis shoes, never moved without a cigarette between her lips, the ascending smoke making her eyes narrow in her wrinkled face.

Margaret was delighted with the smell of oil paint and turps that pervaded the house. The son, Sven, was an artist, she knew. The party took place in half-darkness as the Christmas tree was lighted in authentic Nordic fashion by candles balanced — some precariously — in small holders at the tips of branches. The atmosphere, somehow enriched by the paraffin heater, and by Mrs O's compelling skill as a story-teller, stilled and enthralled even the most blasé among the children. The tales were unfamiliar, full of haunted night-falls among dark woods and the deeds of ill-wishing goblins.

The daughter, Marthe, was plain and silent. She served them with milky coffee and seed-buns, and they giggled at the grown-up tastes, new to them and so different from the usual party fare of orange drinks and jelly.

Then the lights were switched on, the sliding doors to the back room opened, shy old Mr Olsen summoned, and a presentation was staged. Sven had been quick to persuade Mr and Mrs Reidy, from across the road, to commission a portrait of each of their children. The portraits — highly coloured, with a slight mauve tinge, the paint standing out in streaks and lumps — were revealed hanging on the wall of the back room.

Sven introduced Mr and Mrs Reidy. They were somewhat nonplussed, though distracted by the performance of the Olsens, mother and son. But the presence of so many children and a dawning puzzlement as to what had come over them to go along with any part of the plan, discomforted them. They took formal possession of the portraits, to applause.

Years afterwards, Margaret saw that the portraits were still duly displayed in the Reidys' lounge among the Hummel figures and Beleek china. Were they a reminder of how lightly, after all, they had escaped?

After the Reidys had left Sven made a few more forays upstairs, padding rapidly in his soft shoes. His golden hair still showed traces of the comb and a cravat filled the open neck of his snazzy shirt. A car horn sounded outside and it became clear that he had not dressed up merely to impress the Reidys. One of his girlfriends, the full-blown daughter and heiress of a pork-butcher, was calling for him. His mother clasped his head between her palms and stood on tiptoe to kiss him soulfully. He waved to the children and sprang gracefully down the steps to the car.

Though all to her was now anti-climactic, Madame O summoned from the kitchen her daughter, to play the violin for the children. Though Marthe was about as competent a musician as her brother was a painter, she was humble about her gift, and her broad pale face showed relief when her mother instructed her to desist, and let in the first of the smiling, rather sheepish, fathers, who had been sent to collect their children when their wives began to feel that it was getting too late for them to be out, even in a house so near.

Dada was home early that night, and he had a longish chat with Madame O when he arrived for Margaret and William.

"She's certainly an entertaining character," he told Mama later. "According to herself, she was patted on the head by Ibsen when he was returning from the tavern in Oslo and she was on her way to school. Christiana, it would have been at the time."

Feeling the Hogans to be somehow sympathetic, Madame O told them about her theatrical ventures in the basement club theatres of Dublin, her plans to stage *A Midsummer Night's Dream* in Blackrock Park. They had sometimes attended and Dada always tried to get her some publicity. At a high point of her enthusiasm, she confided to Mama the reason why she felt most at home with them.

"I know why you are so happy", she cried, "you are not married."

To her, being married meant encasing love in deadening propriety and instrumental dealing. In that sense, she thought, most people were married: wary of the new, of the possibility of adventure.

It must have been shortly after the party that the Olsens realised the game would soon be up. Sven and Madame O decided a flit was timely. It was, plainly, something they had often done before. At least this time, they didn't have to carry their suitcases down at night, crossing silent squares to the railway station, to sit in the waiting-room till morning. Though the dilemma: what to take, what to leave behind was the same, at least this time they had a bit in hand.

News came out later, after the Olsens' abrupt departure from the road, of how much credit Madame O had been able to wheedle out of the local shops, and how little of the outstanding sum she had paid.

The mood of the road having swung definitely against them, no-one wondered why they had moved out as suddenly as they had moved in. The subject was literally dropped, and it was in any case not long before the house was sold to a civil servant and his family. Dada heard later that Marthe had moved to London, looking after her parents out of her small salary, and that Sven had taken off for the Continent. Quite apart from the creditors, he would probably soon have felt the need to work a different and more lucrative scene than Dublin.

Mention of the portraits after that always brought out a certain tackiness in Mrs Reidy's tone. "We feel it was a good investment," she told Mrs Murphy.

But Mrs Murphy's comment to Mrs Breen seemed eloquent, tinctured with satisfaction. "The frames are extra, of course."

Mama's friend, Marie, worked in the Sweep. She called to see Mama and had her tea on Mondays. Mr Joe McGrath was mentioned in the papers as in the past year two of his horses, Solar Slipper and Sammy's Rock, had won big money prizes in England.

"He's rolling in money, anyway," Mama said. "He doesn't need the prizes."

"It's people like him should have money," Marie insisted.

"Look at all the employment he gives to working girls."

They were called girls because they were not married, though of course widows also made a part of the crowd that streamed across the Ballsbridge zebra crossing, some very tiny, some with irons on their legs, some old and worn.

Every Wednesday night Marie went to St John's Ambulance Brigade classes in advanced first aid, and sometimes she had to attend matches or big meetings in uniform. On Fridays she called to her married sister's and brought sweets to the children whom she looked after for the evening. Her placid life was transformed by a letter from a half-forgotten uncle who had gone to the USA many years before. He wrote in the traditional manner, asking for one of the family to go out and look after him, as he was now in poor health. As the eldest, Marie was clearly the one to take up what everybody thought was a great chance. She would be certain to find a man, and to improve her standing. The reliable woman was so quiet that she almost seemed invisible at times. After Christmas night parties, christenings or funerals, the question was often asked if she had been there. Even when it came to catching groups in photos, she was rarely in them, unless partially in the background. For the first time in her life, she became the centre of attention now that America beckoned. It was assumed that her uncle had lots of money — had he not left home a young man? — and that she would get it when he died. Almost as if it had been a marriage trip, she received presents at a series of evenings, each held in a different house. Her sister and brother-in-law saw her off from Collinstown in a Constellation.

Inevitably, she was more on their minds than they on hers, in the days that followed. The letters came rapidly enough about Rochester. Being in upstate New York, quite far from New York City, she had to explain that the names and addresses she had been given were not really much use till she had more time, maybe on her next vacation. They noticed how quickly she was picking up American words like that.

Her uncle turned out to be in fairly good health but not, apparently, so keen on giving her a home with him unless she

[53]

got a job. She went into an insurance company in town, in the cash department. At least she'll get his money when he dies, they said, after the news that she would not, after all, be kept in comfort — for all her family and friends, the proper condition of a woman. Though knowledge of money and legal matters among the conclave was limited, speculation and opinion reflected the fascination the subject aroused. After some years, the uncle went into a nursing home and Marie soon found that the house would have to be sold to pay the expenses. When, finally, he died, the little money left he had willed to the pastor of St. Anthony's Church, where he had attended nine o'clock Mass every Sunday for forty years.

Marie stayed on in the insurance company. Her promotion was slow but steady. She finally got used to answering people's questions about herself. She really was single, not divorced or separated.

Margaret knew the callers that made each afternoon of the week different from the others: the insurance man, the milkman, the breadman, all of whom got coins or a ten shilling note from the jar on the mantelpiece. But the postman who arrived one spring day in a van and left a large parcel was a novelty.

When Margaret raced into the big bedroom with the form for Mama to sign, she found her lightly set on the window sill near the mirror. Her delicate crossed ankles were free of the floor, her back to the open frame, the garden, the sky.

That was the end of window-cleaning for the day. The soft box was laced with string and stuck with green stamps of the Statue of Liberty. The label said it contained worn clothes. Thinking perhaps that this description hardly sounded enticing, Mama explained quickly.

"Marie has some very rich friends who give her lovely things. She buys a few new clothes, too, God help her."

On Mama's bed the spoils were laid out. Long straight skirts, too wide for Mama, too long for Margaret, shortie pyjamas, and finally, under their protective veil of tissue paper, the hats. They were what Mama called "little hats":

black and white boaters, green velvet caps studded with pearls, stuck with feathers, stiff navy shapes with small clips over the ears to hold them on. Some of the veils had rhinestones, others tiny velvet spots, scattered at intervals.

All of these suited Mama very well, and she loved to wear them going to weddings, into town, to dos that in the year of the first parcel marked the PEN Club Congress. Among the wives she was, everybody said, one of the liveliest and best dressed. The Argentinian Embassy was at that time the leading giver of parties. She danced tangos and quicksteps with the PEN delegate of that country. He was young, with broad shoulders and spaces between his front teeth.

Mr and Mrs Rosenberg looked like an ordinary middle-aged couple in their hats and overcoats. But according to the newspapers they were far from ordinary: Jews, Communists and, worst of all, spies, who during the war had handed America's atom secrets over to the Russians. The American President finally decided that they should be electrocuted in Sing Sing prison. When Ethel Rosenberg had already received as much electricity as had killed her husband, she was still alive. They had to increase the charge until white smoke came out of her head.

As they were brought along the corridor to the room (was it tiled?) where the steel chairs with the leather straps stood, they could surely spare little feeling for the cause they had served (though during the night, in their separate cells, they had sung the 'Internationale') nor for their sons (though they had said goodbye the day before) nor even (lest they break down) for each other, or for anyone besides the guards. With these, the bond was total: there was left the hope that they'd carry out their part, make their move, fasten the straps, quickly.

At Miss Dillon's, during the Christian Doctrine class, someone saw in the question of the Rosenbergs a chance to hold up the work, that day on *Apologetics*. Would they go to Hell? she asked.

"Of course they will, didn't they betray their country?" was Miss O'Rourke's reply.

Other girls, more wily, pressed subtler points. Had the visit of a Rabbi made no difference to their prospects of salvation?

"Outside the True Church, there is no salvation. On Good Fridays we pray for the perfidious Jews, to save them from their blindness and from their Rabbis, who teach them that the Messiah is still to come and that Saturday is a holy day. Our Lord told them that His blood would be upon themselves and on their children."

But Margaret knew that everybody didn't feel that way. Though it made things more puzzling, it was also a kind of relief to know that a painter called Picasso (she always remembered the unfamiliar name) had sent drawings of the Rosenbergs to their sons.

In the games she and William had played long ago with the Murphys, the Reidys and others, if you picked orange juice (instead of a prod of a pin, or best of all, a lick of a cat) you were fair game for sniggers: "You're a Jew. You killed Our Lord."

These games went on, even after a Jewish family had moved to the road. The Levys had, exceptionally, not stuck to the areas usually favoured by prosperous Jews and they didn't seem particularly devout. Their house was extremely comfortable, with a fridge, a chiming door-bell and twin beds in the parents' room.

"They're hard to work for," Dutch had said, "they stick up for each other, and they're always grasping for profit in business." But Margaret thought not of the rag trade in William Street but of the beautiful boys from Park House School, with their rich skin tones, their curly hair, and she knew that her sneaking liking for Jews sprang from feelings that, again, she couldn't fully discern, let alone communicate.

Something stirred in Dutch the idea of making a family tree. As she summoned all the anecdotes the old people had told her, the Hogan saga inspired her with pride and satisfaction. The family stemmed from a John, who as a child had escaped when, in 1798, yeomen spiked the bed in which he lay hidden. Concerning him two facts shone warmly through the subsequent generations, defining the family's course. First, he died beseeching his large family of sons to abstain from politics and to master instead the building trade in which they were already engaged. Secondly, his wife, a non-Catholic as they said, was, through the influence of her youngest son William, persuaded to attend a mission at Duiske Abbey and was converted.

As the family grew and spread, they prospered, as builders, publicans and corn factors. In every generation there were sons and daughters given to the Church. With this family, respectable, circumscribed and rather graceless, Dutch and Dada were out of step. He was by and large indifferent to the matter, but Dutch would have wished to deny, or undo, this sidestep, to correct the drift, to reach back and tap the source of piety and prosperity. For her, this source lay in the branch she knew best: the most complete and exemplary testimony to the family spirit was the Hogan household at St Mullins, home of her cousin John, his wife Kay and their six children.

Margaret remembered calling to their house, especially the first time she had stayed the night. It was autumn and the Virginia creeper on the front of the house was a blur of pinks and yellows. A huge cream-coloured Aga range filled the kitchen with warmth, but the clumsy-looking maid hunted the children of the house, their cousin visitors, and some local children who were always around the place, into the yard. Here, among surprising smells of manure and corn chaff, stood the family's cars: not one but two big Ford Zodiacs. They had travelled down in one of them, and all Margaret's pleasure in the trip had vanished in a lively sense of unfairness when John had put the five-year-old William on his knee to take the wheel for some miles on the quiet roads of West Wicklow. Even before the other horrors of which the country seemed full: the runny bright yellow cow pat that had ruined her shoes, the carnage of small animals in the corn-field during the harvest, she was expecting the worst.

Between the two cars the family were parcelled out to leave in good time for ten o'clock Mass. When they came in with the *Sunday Independent* Kay had big plates of bacon, eggs and white pudding ready, with aromatic tea. They got out the car too, for more casual errands, down to the shops for bottles of orange or packets of biscuits if they ran short. The origins of their wealth, the undertaking business, the mill in town, were plain and solid as the buildings that housed these activities. The Papal Blessing on John and Kay's marriage showed the beaked nose, the delicate features, the intense dark eyes of Pius XII. It hung over the china cabinet in the sitting-room and, together with the praise they got (echoed by Dutch more than once) of John for donating land for church buildings, of Kay for embroidering vestments for the West African Mission, proclaimed their adherence to a code higher than business.

Kay was quite a talented pianist, and sang in the church choir. All of the children had gone to music lessons, and Brendan, the eldest, was thought to show promise.

Margaret liked her cousins well enough, but if someone had said that she resembled them, she would have been amazed and disbelieving, thinking of the girls' washed-out cotton frocks, the boys' wide shorts, the grubbiness of the baby who sat up fastened by fancy leather straps in his pram. But those who said it were quite right. The cousins were, whether she could admit it or not, versions of herself. They represented — and this could have made her start — how she might have turned out if the small step had not been taken. The small step was her grandfather Joseph's doing: he had done it for them and had done for them.

It had begun with an essentially commonplace occurrence. Joseph bungled the timber business he had been given by his father, a particularly solid Hogan (builder of the church at Borris, and of a fine stone house in which he lived with his family). But even among the Hogans others had suffered similar setbacks. What made it different in Joseph's case was that, the business gone, it became clear that he had failed to take the impress made on his brothers and sisters by habit, a sense of duty or fear.

A period spent in Australia did not materially alter his situation, and he returned to live in Rathmines after his marriage, working with what seemed complete indifference in the timber yards of other merchants. Having simply not had the stomach to persist in the way of life offered by his home place, he had put nothing very different in its stead. He still insisted on a goose for Christmas and would not hear of turkey, he occasionally expressed a regret for not having gone in for farming like his younger brother (father of the Uncle John that Margaret visited), a hope to see a grandson before he died, a wish to be buried in his home place. By and large, however, he remained sunny, seemingly untroubled by speculation on what might have been.

The effects of his gesture were incalculable for his descendants. They were, overnight it seemed, separated for ever from the bond of the land, from the family place, from the certainty of living and dying in the midst of familiarity. Unlike him, they were required to improvise, to invent.

The business of making the family tree revealed some of this to Margaret, though indirectly. At the time she appreciated her grandfather's position less than the tangled feelings of the people around her at home: a tangle in which Dutch's wish to inoculate William, Mary, and Margaret with Hogan virtues and values, was somehow a part of Dada's amused half-interest, and a slightly sharp edge in Mama's voice.

One autumn Sunday, when Kilkenny was playing in the All-Ireland Final, a crowd of neighbours gathered in the parlour at St Mullins to listen on the radiogram. Margaret wandered out to the yard. Brendan had his bicycle under him, toe-tips just in contact with the ground.

"Would you like a spin?" he asked, taking one hand off the handle-bar so that she could shift herself up on the bare crossbar. He rushed around the yard, sending hens scuttling for cover, then raced along a boggy lane to the old cemetery, where he wove in and out of the stones, across some of them, sweeping in great curves through the grass. She looked out all the time, ahead, at what hazard, what near miss: gate, wall, cow, stone, was coming up, but she was conscious of his breath, his pumping legs, now like hers, soaked from the long grass. When they stopped, she looked up at him and caught a look of intensity, a set expression on his face. She leaned back against him as, unsmiling, he put his hands on her shoulders, his face down on her hair.

Their trips became more adventurous: down the hill before the village, around the Norman motte, along the quayside, to the curve of the river where the path through the wood led to Ross. They talked little: they were confederates. He knew the whole countryside, about the treatment of greyhounds, and farming, and French kissing. Yet she knew, in some way, that Brendan envied her, as she certainly envied him.

Almost from the beginning, the new magazine had not gone well for Dada. He had begun it with a particular kind of reader in mind, the people whose desire for information about the older smart set would not be fully satisfied by the Social and Personal Column in the *Irish Times*, reporting the arrivals and departures at the Russell and the Hibernian. Irishmen who had made money during the Emergency would want to know about the leaders of fashion or anyway their wives would: they would want to see themselves in the same pages. Here appeared the Joint Master of the Scarteens, the four sisters of a Mayo judge, now working in New Jersey, the weddings of doctors in the Honan Chapel, UCC, the wife of the Minister of Finance with the Begum Aly Khan, the Tipperary and Midleton show, the daughter-in-law of the ex-Regent of Hungary, the mother of the Bishop of Galway, the debs at Queen Charlotte's Birthday Ball. Here was news of swanky restaurants in New York, the Paris collections, bridge, dog shows, receptions at the embassies, child studies by a new photographer in Monkstown. Dada had a penchant for style and grace that had not been satisfied at Synge Street, in the National Movement or the Abbey Theatre. He could locate what he admired only in the British upper class and their Irish connections and counterparts. In the post-war England of fuel shortages, rising taxes and death duties, that class was threatened by the levelling spirit of the age. But in Ireland their style of life seemed a more feasible proposition. Food and domestic help were still cheap, elegant big houses were still maintained. The Irish people they came across seemed accustomed to asking little for themselves, as if smart people's interest in the country was flattering or advantageous to them.

To produce a really high-class product, Dada insisted on the best paper, photography and artwork. He had columns on travel, wine and motoring, as well as theatre and art, and liberal coverage of the social round. But net sales were low. As the businessman backing the venture said, you get nothing from the hunting crowd. What really counted were the advertising figures, and you had to chase them up. Yet Patrick continued to believe that the next month's issue would see an upturn in circulation and advertising revenue, while maintaining the tone of the publication. New ads came: His Master's Voice, Dubtex Slacks, Marjorie Boland Mantles, Victor Waddington Galleries, and the Ponds Cold Cream series of Irish Beauties.

When he was thinking of putting a large photo of the daughter of a Meath squire as frontispiece of one Christmas number, Dutch disagreed. "A nice picture of the Holy Mother and Child would be much more suitable. After all, 95% of the population is Catholic. The *Independent* always has a colour photo of the Pope and the Christmas scene."

The recurring worry of the monthly figures was preying even on Dada, an easy-going man. After a bout of flu, he didn't seem to be getting better, and developed unusual symptoms. He began to pass large quantities of urine that gave off a sweet smell like apples. He felt continually thirsty and weary. One morning he stubbed his little toe against the foot of his bed. When he returned, limping, that evening, his toes were black and red streaks ran up his ankle.

"Polyuria, glycosuria and polydipsia," said the specialist, "add up to diabetes mellitus. The threatened gangrene of the foot confirms it."

The condition that the ancients had accurately described as honeyed syphon had only fairly recently been rendered liable to treatment by insulin. It was suspected that the beta cells of the islets of Langerhans in the pancreas were insidiously, gradually, under attack from the body's own white blood cells. Once the production of insulin by the pancreas was affected, sugar would accumulate in the blood and be excreted in the urine without providing nutrition to the muscles. The grape-apple smell of Patrick's breath, his by now frequent resort to sucking sweets, signified the failure of whole systems in his body.

"There's no cure — the treatment simply restores the carbohydrate metabolism to as near as normal as possible," continued the specialist, "he will have to have an injection of insulin every day and follow a strict diet."

Despite its late onset, his diabetic condition was not of the milder variety. It proved hard to stabilise, and a job with lots of worry, late hours and deadlines was quite unsuitable. When he gave up the magazine job, however, worry was redoubled: how, now, to provide for the family?

Many secondary effects followed. His skin became papery, dry and harsh because of the sugar deposited by his sweat. For him a boil or skin ailment, no matter how trivial, had risks of serious complications. The condition swung between two poles, two kinds of danger: a coma due to too much insulin and too little sugar, or the reverse. Mama and Dutch were painstaking in reckoning how much insulin he should get each morning. But because of a dietary indiscretion, an emotional upset, or whatever, he often had insulin shock, or hypoglycaemic coma. Here, the fall in blood sugar concentration brought on a sinking feeling, giddiness, and a moist cold skin. Quite suddenly, he would start breathing shallowly, he would be looking for more food after a large breakfast, and they would have to bring him round with quantities of sugar.

Margaret was called on to make pots of strong tea, her hands shaking as she performed the gestures with caddy, spoon and teapot that were unfamiliar to her but that her mother repeated often, in a day, in a week. Coming upstairs with a cup of the stuff, fortified with a double measure of sugar, she longed, yet feared, to see Dada. He looked at her as if he were seeing double, strangely nervous for so placid and gentle a man, and he seemed confused, not sure of the outside world. Insisting on getting up, he would start, then break off preparations to go out, and start doing something else.

Mama's pleas would eventually recall him: "Patrick, love, darling, take a sip, please take some tea."

To know whether he was responding quickly, not heading into a convulsion, not in a state that required intravenous sugar in hospital, they had to repeatedly check the sugar in his urine. They pondered the liquid in the test-tube. Ten drops of water, five of urine. It boiled and changed colour when the copper sulphate tablet was added. Dutch and Mama sometimes argued, there in the kitchen, out of earshot of Patrick's bedroom, not over the result of the Clinitest — the reassuring yellow, the fairly hopeful orange were very different from the ominous red — but over what the results could mean. Each was dogmatic about what was required.

"It'll go the other way if he doesn't get more insulin."

"Nonsense, he needs a big breakfast at once."

At Mount Argus was the shrine of a Belgian Passionist who was a Servant of God, meaning that he would next attain beatification. It was famous as a spot where special favours could be obtained. Dutch had heard of Father Charles' efficacy in cases that had seemed hopeless. Patrick was, they thought, too tired to go, but the rest of the family made a trip there one Sunday. Duch admired the high iron gates, the massiveness of the stone buildings, and the beauty of the shrine itself, edged with gold, constructed in marble of three different colours. Before it stout ladies, their coats higher at the back than at the front, headscarves pulled tight over their frizzy hair, prayed that their sons or husbands would give up the drink, would get steady work, would start to be good-living again: and young fathers with Brylcreem on their hair prayed that their baby's colic, their toddler's asthma, would be cured.

Outside in the drive, a lady with a black bag clutched against her coat listened to one of the priests of the community as he shrugged his cloak back from his shoulders and adjusted the crucifix that was stuck at an angle in his substantial leather belt. His dark hair was combed straight back from a lowish forehead and some hairs, also dark, sprouted from his short nose and the beginning of his broad fingers.

Dutch transferred from the showrooms of the garment manufacturers to travel as their country representative. Though she might be tired, rushing to make another town before night, yet in sparsely populated areas she never failed to stop and pick people up on the road. The woman — soft, middle-aged, laden with shopping — whom she met one evening on the road between Crossmolina and Ballina, explained that she was hurrying back to the children, who helped her do most of the work on their small farm, as her husband was on an evening shift in the factory outside Ballina. Dutch insisted on taking her the whole way home when she heard of their circumstances. It seemed a long way, by a road springy with the bog that underlay its surface, winding along a ridge that encircled the lower slopes of the mountain and finally went straight into a trackless scrub, where the hardy low-lying vegetation seemed to swallow it up.

Just before their cottage the road did in fact peter out, as Dutch realised too late when, to the accompaniment of the woman's copious apologies, the van stuck in the soft ground. There was nothing to do except wait there in the house with the children till their father should return from Ballina. He would know how to get the van out, they were sure.

Unused to visitors, the Ryan children came shyly forward to greet Dutch. She showed a simplicity that was like their own: less a matter of entering into their world than of bringing them into hers. Her misunderstandings of their soft tones, of their Western accents, delighted them. They were left with a vivid but confusing impression of an adult such as they had never seen before, of a large figure, clad throughout in an overcoat despite the turf fire in the small room, of make-up worn with a fur hat, of cigarettes held in beringed fingers, of a bag bursting with powder compacts, tissues, biros, sales dockets and much more. Their plain, strenuous existence had been touched by something as strange as if it had been a fairy, in the conventional disguise of an old woman, who had appeared at their fireside, or a bear (really a prince) who had knocked at their door, bolted against the winter night. So gauche at times, on other social occasions, she was here in command, able to transform the chance encounter into something unique, enriching in a way that could hardly be described. It was dark when the father arrived, and by revving the van more forcefully than Dutch ever would, he reversed it back onto the road and went with her till she found again the turn for Ballina.

In other random encounters, too, Dutch touched and won people. She was able to find and confide in French people, and she corresponded with many that she had met on holidays. The closest was a lady like herself, middle-aged, regarded as eccentric, pious, holding herself aside from many things about the modern world.

She took Dutch to visit the streets around the Sacré Coeur, where she looked shyly over the painters' shoulders as they worked at their canvasses or haggled about the prices. The endless variations they produced on corners of the Place du Tetre with its flower stalls, or studies of wistful dogs or children, prompted Dutch to try, in a little drawing-pad, to paint water-colours of Connemara lakes and cottages.

She put all these drawings away in shoe-boxes that filled her dressing-table drawers. One Sunday, when it was dark already at midday, she lit a fire in her room. At once, the children wanted to know the reason for such an unusual step.

"I'm going to clear out my drawers, and I'll burn some of

the rubbish."

"Please, can we help you please?"

Dutch could never refuse, but she always had to murmur a bit. "You mustn't jeer, now."

Once the curtains could be drawn on the sad evening outside, the pink, strange-smelling room was cosy. Before Dutch could stop them, William and Margaret had emptied the drawers onto her bed. From among the golf tees, the Sweep tickets and the cards of thread for mending stockings, they pounced on the older-looking snaps, the edges dinged. Young men wearing heavy suits, socks and shoes, despite the bright sunshine, sat with their legs straight in front of them, ankles crossed, on rocks where they had climbed to pose. Girls wore turbans and floral dresses or swimsuits. Pretending to fall around with laughter at the styles, Margaret and William giggled. "Who are they?"

"I'm not sure of all their names now, I used to pal with them years ago."

A postcard from Lough Derg showed people saying the Rosary in bare feet and overcoats. The women had hats. On the back, Dutch's cousin Kay had assured her that she had prayed for her on the pilgrimage. Dutch thought that only prayer could keep a girl from yielding to the temptation of concupiscence, could strengthen her to give up a young man who was a Protestant, like Leslie.

The photo of Dutch dancing with Leslie was taken at the Lady Captain's Dinner at Woodbrook. Only his wrist touched the back of her dress: he held his fingers out stylishly. Margaret remembered him calling to the house, to bring Dutch to the Capitol or the Savoy for the pictures and tea afterwards, or to the DGOS season at the Gaiety. But there had been something about why he and Dutch would no longer be seeing each other: an awkward silence had followed Margaret's enquiry about Dutch's boyfriend. It occurred to Margaret to wonder why so many aunts had loved men who died young of TB, or in the war, and had spent their lives palling with groups of girls, going to business, close to their families, yet independent; like Mrs Murphy's sister, who was always ready to give one of her neighbours a lift, as long as it suited them to get off at Clare Street: because of the traffic, she never took her Anglia any farther.

Something held the children back from jeering Dutch about Leslie. She put the picture into a newly cleared drawer, without comment.

But she didn't mind them looking at the holy pictures she had kept from her First Communion day. Her mother had brought her to the big convent at the end of their road in Rathmines. The women the nuns looked after had gathered around. Their gray hair was very wavy, their teeth bad, their legs veined and thickened. Even in winter, they wore summer dresses and sandals.

"They told me I looked very holy in my white dress, and asked me to pray for them."

"Why did they ask you that?"

"They used to lead very impure lives, William, and the nuns looked after them, and helped them make up for their sins."

Dutch felt she had said too much and was glad when they picked up a photo of Patrick with his Synge Street class. Despite the thick boots, the cropped hair, his good looks made him easy to identify.

She had kept also sadder mementoes: his letters (passed by the Army Censor) from Ballykinlar Internment camp that told her of concerts, of skits, of German lessons, of chess games, trying with cheerful news to wipe out the memory of the night he was arrested. But Dutch knew it would never leave her, the image of how he was hustled down the stairs by RIC men as she stood in the hall looking up.

She proudly showed the children Abbey programmes where his name featured among the small parts. She sometimes wished he had continued as an actor, though it was not a very secure way of life: his voice and his feeling for words put him ahead of most of the ones on the stage nowadays. At weddings he sang, 'Believe me, if all those endearing young charms' and 'The Moon hath raised her lamp above'. The postcards he and his bride had sent from Switzerland carried dates from the last weeks of summer, the last weeks of peace. He was everywhere among her papers: in a cowboy shirt at the hut with Jim and Noel, in evening dress and a chain of office at various functions, publicity and newspaper dos, leaning on the white railings at the RDS, a raincoat over his arm.

The bundles of paper Dutch threw on the fire made soft formations, changed colour dramatically before collapsing, the incandescent unified mass becoming sooty flakes. The fire sizzled when she added some of the little twists of hair (whose, she had not been able to distinguish) and as Margaret and William left, the small fireplace was the source of a sharp, acrid smell, and a scene of activity in the dark room.

Shortly before Margaret left for France, Dutch had a chat with her. She got around to telling her about a woman she knew of who gave birth to an infected child because her husband had caught a dreadful disease before his marriage. To Margaret, it seemed like some kind of caution, though it was difficult to be sure: like the sin the women in the convent had committed, the disease was vague.

That chat also let Margaret know how worried Dutch was about her leaving to spend a year in a foreign country, even if the family had been recommended by a Jesuit priest from Leeson Street. The most recent photo to go into Dutch's drawer was also sent to Margaret, in France. It showed her in her belted camel coat with Mama and Dada, just before her departure.

They had rung Margaret on Christmas night to remind her of the family's customary way of spending the feast. It never varied from one year to the next, except that a different one of Patrick's bachelor friends might come for the dinner. Dutch wrote that Margaret was certain to be comforted by hearing that in spite of her absence and Dad's frequent exhaustion, everything was just the same that year.

Margaret was planning to go to the university after her year in France and, as Dutch said, she hoped that she would concentrate on meeting and going out with someone nice.

III

"THE WOOD AROUND here is called Compiegne," they said, and for Margaret the name held the very essence of France: the Hundred Years War, the Armistice signed twice, in a railway carriage, and Joan of Arc taken. Above all, there was a scene from the *Book of Hours*: flower-studded meadows, delicate stags and does, lords and ladies in chase.

The greetings and unloading were hurried when they reached Dubois'. Margaret was given a large panelled bedroom with a marble wash-stand and fat china ewers in the corner. Claudine, the eldest, explained that there was no hot water upstairs, she would bring it up in the morning. When Margaret wakened, excitement quickly followed the confusion of the first moments. Looking out, she saw no sign of the wood. Instead, flat, pale countryside, a river, mist-coiled, locked immobile between its banks, poplars outlining the road.

At dinner that night she studied the family. Though she spoke French quite well, the delays and gaps that were accepted as natural, together with a certain reserve in the Dubois, gained for her the chance to observe. Compared with her brothers, Claudine was quite attractive. They and the small sister had something feral about their black brows, pointed noses and sloping chins. The boys' skulls were peculiarly shaped: their foreheads bulged, their crowns were flattened. Though these features ran through the family, they seemed to peter out, so that the younger boys showed them most, the elder least. Did they gradually grow out of it, she wondered, looking at M. Dubois' quite shapely skull, covered with a strong silver crew-cut.

He was a sinewy, elastic man, with big joints. It was probably the second evening that he suddenly struck one of the boys on the forehead with a plate. The blow came without much warning, though he did snap out a brief phrase, which Margaret didn't catch, just as the plate broke in two and fell on the table.

Mme. Dubois was placid, and her colourlessness somehow belied her rich brown hair and russet skin. The small girl set off by bicycle to school before Margaret was up, and returned at the moment when the roast beef had succeeded the soup on the rush mat in the centre of the table. Her scrawny body looked lost in her school blouse and she had enormous mauve circles under her eyes. The children's schooling seemed to be taken very seriously. Claudine made little use of hers, however. Her days were spent in helping her mother and running Scout meetings, in a forage cap and dress loaded with lanyards and badges.

Margaret savoured the delicious condition of those who need not answer for anything just at that moment. She was en route to somewhere else.

The Dubois' cousins, who were to be her French family for the year, lived further to the north. In the photos Claudine showed her, the de Thierrys, especially Anne, were shown shooting and riding in the woods. It was a family of daughters, except for Maurice, the eldest. Like M. Dubois, Maurice wore breeches, gaiters or ribbed woollen stockings and jackets of corduroy or leather. Margaret had seen such clothes only in books; in Ireland, farmers wore grey city trousers and rubber boots.

As the train moved through the yard of the station at Amiens, Margaret tugged at her cases on the rack. A middle-aged man helped her to bring them into the corridor, past soldiers burdened with kitbags and country women with blue-checked aprons, headscarves and boots.

It was Anne who waited on the platform: impossible to mistake her athletic bearing. After the beetling Dubois she seemed a golden princess. Margaret reckoned that she would use more English there, as Anne greeted her in an accent straight from the Irish midlands. Madame and Lucienne were waiting in the car: Madame was an older version of Anne: upswept hair that was kept blonde, a figure that was still slim despite twelve pregnancies. Lucienne was brown-haired, with narrow features, somewhat in the Dubois style. Margaret waved her thanks to the man from the train.

"Do you know him?"

Margaret sensed their disapproval, but not the reason.

The avenue curved so that the house was not visible until one was almost on it. For a chateau it was more modest than Margaret had expected, with two long rows of windows and their opened-back shutters. To the front stretched a green sward, then the woods, the main source of income, began. At the back a cobbled yard was framed with outhouses, and a long kitchen garden climbed up a low hill. Not realising how much Margaret understood Madame asked, through Anne, about their new guest's family. The word came back: the latest Irish girl was the daughter of a journalist.

The two sisters who came between Anne and Lucienne were preparing lunch. In looks, too, Marie-Paule and Marie-Claire were midway. Though blonde, they lacked Anne's radiance, and the visible down on their faces was a blemish, Margaret thought. Two daschunds grunted in sleep before an immense fireplace. She ate carrots as she had never seen them before: raw, grated and covered with oil and vinegar; it seemed strange that they were served by themselves. Then came fish fried in butter, cheese and oranges. They owed this rather sumptuous lunch to Margaret's arrival and the fact that Madame had been in town.

Jacqueline, the youngest, was home from boarding-school with flu.

"Did you get her the suppositories, Maman?" Lucienne took the celluloid cylinders, and some impish spirit prompted her to show them to Margaret.

"Look at the size of them."

Hoping to respond correctly, Margaret murmured something about how did one swallow them. Her gaffe brought peals of laughter, and even Madame smiled before explaining with the aid of a dictionary.

From the room beside her own, which connected by a door, Margaret heard comments not meant for her to understand.

"Elle est moche."

The dictionary again. Moche meant a fright, especially of appearance. It was her first exposure to the kind of criticism the girls made so freely, sitting in the car after shopping in town or discussing a party. She had always assumed she looked all right. *Moche.* Now she longed for hollower cheeks, finer hands. Her mother had thought her well-equipped for a winter stay in France, with hats, mittens, bootees and belted camel coat. But she only wanted to look like the girls did, in a jumper and skirt with a silk headscarf.

In the smaller section of the house lived Maurice, his wife Béatrice, and their baby with her nurse. After lunch on that first day Béatrice appeared. She had a longish, oval face, a face from the *Book of Hours*, beautiful, narrow feet and hands, and she was much more soignée even than Madame, whom she called *ma mère*. The visits of their young sister-in-law were trying for the girls. Marie-Paule was engaged to Guy de Belleville, Béatrice's brother, and each family thought that their alliances did the other greater honour. But secretly the De Thierrys rejoiced in Béatrice's pretentiousness. They could even forgive her the hideous little Chihuaha dog that had to be rescued each time from the daschunds' feigned ferocity, though not the fact that she brought him more than twice as often as she brought her daughter. Like Madame, Béatrice had her hand kissed, not shaken, by men of breeding. As wife of the only son, she seemed to move in a more exalted sphere: Madame and the girls had maids only occasionally: Béatrice never did housework.

Though there was, at the most, one day a week when they worked hard, the afternoons, thought Margaret afterwards, always moved at the slow pace of a lesson. Margaret's inexperience was compounded by Lucienne's distaste for effort, and this could be contagious. As the fire became a tissue of grey ash, enfeebled by the low sun, they would move to the radiator sooner than fetch wood. As they now had a view from the window, they could sooner or later call to Henri to bring in a load. His scolding and Lucienne's protestations could take up fifteen minutes. Now nearly sixty, with a round head and a white cascade of moustache, Henri still looked like a soldier of the 1914-18 war, which had, for the first and only time, brought him from his village.

Their first plan was made in enthusiasm: to go right through the programme for English and French of the final year in school. Rabelais seemed the right place to start and together they looked at the pages listing his life, works and reputation. They hardly knew what to do next with such a catalogue and the language of the extracts defeated them. The prescribed book in English was *Middlemarch*, also parcelled out in extracts, with notes explaining references to the Reform Bill and Evangelical churchmen.

Once the preparations for the afternoon snack, the *goûter*, began — and some days this was very early indeed — the lesson was thankfully abandoned. The girls were not uncultivated: they read Dostoevsky and William Faulkner and took piano lessons. In time, discussion (in French) of Lucienne's reading and occasional translation of the words of a song by the Platters became the only work required of Margaret. She found a hoard of Penguins in a cupboard in the older bathroom and from then on watched for the chance to slip up to the huge airy attic where the washing was hung and where she could read and dream. She saw herself, now soignée, setting out herbs to dry and apples to ripen on boards in an outhouse, sorting fragrant sheets in deep drawers, checking the returns from timber or sugar-beet and oiling and waxing fine oak floors.

After *goûter* they often walked in the falling evening to the village. These excursions had often no other purpose than to catch sight of a local boy, Roger, whom Lucienne insisted she loved. In fantasy she was a rebel against the marriages which Madame would arrange for each of them. She told Margaret that Anne too was in love, but that her mother would not let her marry Eric.

"Why not?"

"Because his is not a good family. They made lots of money since the war."

"What will Anne do?"

"She'll go to Paris and be an air-hostess, and so shall I."

"When?"

"Next year, for sure. I'll write to you when I got to Paris."

Some reciprocal confidence seemed demanded. Margaret received letters now and then from an uninteresting dental student who had gone to Canada. She exaggerated her involvement with him, to Lucienne: delays in the post were a useful way of explaining bad humour.

This time of short days and rain that turned the fine clays into mud was a dead season for work outdoors. Instead, Henri attended to chores around the yard. The walks were often the most enjoyable moment of the day. Even the iron cold and blackness could be thrilling in contrast to a kitchen lit and heated by oil, where in the smelly golden warmth a child sat doing homework in a squared copybook.

If, on the road, they happened to hear, marvellously, the sound of a motocyclette, they would stand still by the hedge until they had seen who it was. Lucienne was convinced always that it would be Roger, but he never came.

On an unfamiliar stretch of road, near a village they rarely entered, Lucienne's flashlight fell on a huge crucifix. Her father had been murdered here just before the liberation of the region. The killer was now the mayor of the village up ahead. Having settled an old score, he had never looked back in his pursuit of power. For Madame and her children, the version authorised by speeches and dedications each succeeding November was a lie. Their remembrance was to visit the tomb beside the church where, three months before Jacqueline's birth, Charles de Thierry had been buried.

The evening walks had sometimes the pretext of a message for Madame. Josette lived nearest to the chateau. Her blue overall was skimpy over her huge body. Margaret rarely followed what she said; her delivery was chesty and she and Robert, her husband, used the Picard dialect. Innumerable invaders had left deposited in the speech of the place words of English, Flemish and German, just as they had left their bones and their weapons under the wide fields. Robert lifted his cap to scratch his head, cut slices from a vast cake of bread he held to his chest, and took swallows from a glass of *pinard*. Their house stank of stale wine and there were times that Josette had to take refuge at the chateau when his mood turned violent. She could claim this sanctuary as a right. She was Madame's neighbour, like the village children who came to the chateau every Thursday for a catechism lesson on their free day from school.

Most people there were anticlerical: that is to say, they rarely went to Mass. They differed little in other ways from the believers, fearing the State as they had once feared the Church. For them, the postman who brought the family allowances was what the *Curé* had been: the representative of a remote and incomprehensible authority. Faced with more fearful realities, they had to rely on the propitiatory gestures of an earlier time. They hung flints in the stables to protect animals and scared their children into obedience with tales of Gargantua.

The church had a slated tower and a gilt vane around which birds wheeled and clacked. On Sundays when the girls took their places around the organ, which Madame played, they would have as fellow-worshippers only a few of the catechism class, two of whom (white woollen habits corded tightly around their stout waists) would rattle through the

[77]

responses as servers, a varying number of newly bereaved families and youths home from National Service in Algeria.

One Sunday, Jules came to make his thanksgiving and greeted Madame after Mass. He was a stocky youth with a heavy backside and short legs. His hair was crisply waved, his eyes lazy and bold. His return somehow created a stir; it meant there was another man about the place. It was at that time too that the war appeared to move closer. Marie-Paule was especially jittery about her fiancé, Guy de Belleville, still over there in Algeria. The post was slow and often disrupted by strikes.

The preparations for Christmas centred on entertaining guests. The silver was painted with a milky liquid which had to be wiped off immediately, necessitating squads of helpers working at once. Attics were transformed into bedrooms, unseen dinner services produced from cupboards, moss collected in the woods for a crib that was set up beside the fireplace. But shopping had its place, too. The girls, laughing, took Madame's purse so that they could buy her a present. In Amiens, the pastry shops sparkled with exquisite treats: macaroons in tall glass jars, thin chocolate mints in gold paper, marrons glacés in wooden boxes, delicately curved almond tuiles in round tins. And behind the columns where these stood, mirrors broke up and multiplied the images over and over. The blank modern boulevards and the steep ancient streets that led straight to the cathedral were crowded.

Now the riches of the cellar were sampled and brought forth. The boiled eggs and milk soups of the past months, though served with more style than the Irish fry, began to look frugal beside the Reveillon supper menu that recalled the days of Bonne-Maman, the mother of Madame. The turkey, so important in Margaret's other Christmasses, was absent. In its place were sucking pig from the spit, Bayonne ham, chickens in elaborate garnishes of jelly. Marie-Claire's speciality was the *Buche de Noel*. This cake was concocted of chestnut, butter and eggs, sweetened with rum and covered with chocolate icing, scored with wavy lines to simulate bark. After Midnight Mass in a convent, they gathered to welcome

Christmas in the company of their guests, who included Béatrice's family, Madame de Belleville and her younger son, Giles.

They were dancing in the salon when the phone call came for Margaret. There was so much noise which she could not silence that time was lost trying to catch her parents' words. She later heard that the call had been horribly expensive. It had only pointed up her apartness from the de Thierrys without closing the distance from home. After she had hung up, she went back to the table and took more, and then more, of the *Buche de Noel*. Only Madame noticed it and the touch of her hand was a pledge of sympathy. Next day the girls teased her about all the anisette she had drunk and all the boys that had kissed her, but the kindness behind the fibs was harder to bear than malice.

There was a maid at the chateau: a cheeky little Basquaise, who fancied Jules. One afternoon streaming with rain she was doing the ironing, piling neatly the pants they changed daily and the long corsets Madame wore. Margaret and Lucienne were called from the lesson to help pull and fold the sheets. Though it was still early, Jules, not Henri, arrived with the milk. He had held onto bits of his uniform: short boots, khaki drill trousers and a cape for the rain. His hands looked pink and raw from the damp air. Madame and the three older girls were, exceptionally, out for the afternoon. Realising they were alone in the house, Jules relaxed, perched on the edge of the table, produced cigarettes. Lucienne and the maid started to joke about the *forêt vierge*, fixing their eyes on the part of his trousers where the drill was stretched tight as he sat on the table. Margaret was suddenly emboldened and it was she who asked, almost dreamily, "Are there giraffes in the virgin forest?" while she too stared at his fat thighs and above. That she would be the most outspoken, the funniest, was a surprise, even to herself. It was easy, after all, to belong, to enter the circle. From that time it was assumed that Jules and she "got on well together", as they put it.

Madame always liked to bring Jules along on trips to the cinema in case of a puncture on the road. He sat beside

Margaret as they watched *War and Peace*. She felt that, like Natasha, she could love a melancholy Prince Andre or a seeker after truth like Pierre. But when Jules came into her mind, he always looked as she had seen him once in the poultry yard in the act of wringing the neck of a duck whose outspread wings were clamped, one under each of his knees.

Early in the New Year, Margaret and Lucienne were to go and see Miss, who had been governess to older members of the family. They set off on two sorry-looking bicycles disastrously lacking in gears. Leaving the familiar country, they headed east to where, long since, the woods had been cut back and huge fields of sugar-beet stretched, dark and monotonous. It was a place made for battles where the armies of Henri IV, Louis XIII and Maréchal Foch had fought. Crossing the river Somme, at a point nearly midway between Thiepval and Vermandouvillers, Margaret thought of her uncle, killed on the Somme in 1916. Half a million of the clerks, artisans and small farmers of Europe had perished there. In innumerable villages, monuments glorified their sacrifice (made in defence of hearth and children, mothers and wives) and solicited later generations to follow. Was that what they had meant? Or was it their secret that the call-up had been a chance they grabbed at to escape from villages, from hearth and children, mothers and wives?

Miss was a dry sandy-haired little woman. When they sat around the fire after tea, Margaret was surprised to see Miss hitch up her skirt and open her legs. After nearly forty years in France, Miss still took milk in her tea and spoke with the accents of Chiswick; but England had become remote too, the memory of it fed now only by her sister's letters and the *Cercle Anglais* that met in Amiens. They even managed an Anglican service twice a year. But, with the passage of time, the circle had shrunk. A trip home was out of the question when even the newspapers had become so expensive.

Miss had been diligent, kind but firm with her charges. She had put them through the masters of English literature and the history of the British Empire. She had not shrunk from drilling them in the phrasal verbs. Nor had the families she had worked for been ungrateful. One or other always asked her to spend Christmas with them, and they would meet her at the station in their big black cars or shooting-brakes. She would give them the dried flower arrangement she had made and hear how many children, or how many acres, had been added since last she saw them.

Miss had met most of the Irish girls who had stayed with Madame. They arrived as she had, dazzled by what they knew of France, secretly touched by the hope of marrying a handsome gentleman. But Miss would never admit to a similarity of the kind. To her, Ireland was a place of no interest, a land of rebellion and unruly drinking. Privately, too, she never considered their qualifications adequate.

The way home was mostly downhill. Their muscles twitching with fatigue, their eyes stinging in the bitter wind, Margaret and Lucienne were unconcerned to notice the tiny abandoned hut, once the shelter of a village shepherd, which was the only man-made thing for miles.

Once in the course of the winter the de Thierrys would travel to confession to M. le Curé, at Ailly le Haut Clocher. On arriving there Madame would call first on the Voisin family. They lived in a dishevelled cottage with a wild weedy garden where they greeted Madame with toothless smiles. There was a great-grandmother, grandmother, mother and daughter, none of whom had ever been married, and none of whom mentioned any man by name. On the way home the girls discussed whether the daughter was already pregnant in her turn.

"She's expecting, Maman, I swear she's expecting."

The Voisins cheerfully swept M. le Curé's few rooms and the church where they brought each new member of the family for christening.

M. le Curé was a little old man with simian features. They sat in his living room where his supper still lay on the table. He was too old to go into the unheated church at night, so the confession took place there, with the penitent kneeling on a *prie-dieu* beside his chair. When Margaret's turn came she was nervous at having him see her so clearly, at using

French. When she began, in her usual low tones, the prayers Madame had taught her earlier, further complications emerged: M. le Curé was quite deaf.

The trip had a double purpose: as well as the absolution, M. le Curé supplied them with honey. This time they took a dozen pots. It was solid, the colour of greyish sand. The girls broached one pot before going to bed, thickly coating scraps of toast with the delicious paste until the pot was empty. As they were parting at the top of the stairs, Lucienne giggled. "I heard every word you said to M. le Curé." Margaret couldn't be sure whether it was more of Lucienne's teasing, so she did not reply. But her dreams that night were troubled yet exciting. The four Voisins plied her with honey from a spoon as they caressed their own bodies and swayed backwards and forwards, murmuring, "It feels good, doesn't it?" through their gappy mouths.

Lucienne had evidently got it wrong about Anne's marriage. In a struggle that had never been visible to Margaret, Anne had somehow carried the day. She was as determined as Madame and much younger: she and Eric were to be married at the end of May.

Absorbed as they were in trips to dressmakers and hairdressers, the de Thierry family could not remain untouched by the rumour and panic of that time. All through the spring housewives bought up stocks of coffee and tinned food, as hysterical gangs of *Algérie Francaise* youths demonstrated in Oran.

"Never stand beside an Algerian in a bus," Lucienne had warned.

"They shoot a drug into you and you wake up as a white slave."

Margaret shivered if she saw an Algerian peddling a pile of carpets in the street, or if they passed one of the tiny harshly-lit cafes from which Arab music floated at every hour.

Maurice had been a paratrooper in Indochina. He explained to his mother and sisters how strongly the army felt.

"I know when the lads have had enough."

The name of De Gaulle was heard more and more. One wet

day in Amiens they saw a small group of antifascist demonstrators, arms linked, advancing along a boulevard where a row of belted and helmeted police waited in silence. In a side street, barely in view, stood gleaming dark police-trucks.

Two days before their church marriage, Anne and Eric went to the *mairie* for the civil ceremony. Madame's elder daughters, their husbands and children had all arrived: the house was in confusion, with beds for visitors set up in every corner. From the linen store where she had been sent, Margaret went through a connecting door into a little box-room. A camp-bed was unfolded there and it held Anne and Eric; they were lying outside the cover and he was asleep. He wore the riding breeches and boots in which he had walked on the pilgrimage to Notre Dame de Liesse that afternoon, and he was beautiful. "He's very tired," whispered Anne, then she added "Nobody knows we're back from the pilgrimage."

"I won't tell them," and they smiled at each other. Margaret went out the way she had come.

The girls and Madame were never without dress-making or knitting on hand, and Margaret was prompted to begin knitting a jumper. As the date for her return drew nearer, she hurried to finish a task she had grown to hate but stubbornly chose not to abandon. On the fine evenings after Anne's departure the girls leafed through back numbers of *Elle*. They searched for patterns, recipes and, especially, funny letters in the agony columns, which they read aloud. Margaret knew that she had only to ask Madame for help and Madame would at once leave down the solid wooden egg and the sock she was darning on it. But Margaret saw the jumper as past redemption. It had been unravelled so many times that the pale blue wool had lost its beauty. The shoulder seaming was clumsy and gave it a squared look. Lucienne was always asking her questions like: "Are you really ever going to wear it?" Anticipating a trap, no matter how she answered, Margaret shrugged in silence. There were days when Lucienne went to further lengths: "At your age, you'd better start learning to knit and run a house. I pity your husband, the poor slob. If you ever get a husband, that is."

Margaret had stopped being meek. "So what if I never knit a jumper again? I can do without a husband, too."

But they all laughed. "Irish girls are mad."

Just before Margaret left, the news was that Josette's daughter was pregnant and that Jules was to marry her. Their adolescence had been brief and now it was over.

Béatrice wanted to buy a layette in Paris for the baby she was expecting later that summer, so Maurice would drive Margaret on the first leg of her journey home.

Once out upon the *Nationale*, which led straight to Paris, Margaret began to smile to herself.

That autumn, Lucienne replied to Margaret's letter about the university scholarship she had won.

Margaret did not doubt that Lucienne was genuinely glad, but guessed that she had another motive in writing, also. She wanted to tell her the news of her engagement to Giles de Belleville.

IV

THE DISTINCTIVE BLACK
stone was everywhere. Rising abruptly at one end of Prince's
Street was the Castle, a drum of grey. At the other, the blunt
shape of Arthur's Seat. The feeling Margaret had had at the
airport, of sharp east winds, of pale northern skies, was in-
tensified. But between the two landmarks ran the band of
comfortable tea-rooms, of solidly elegant shops with twin
sets and plaid skirts in the windows.

She found Heather's house in Claremount Crescent easily
enough. It was unexpectedly true to its name, a delicate
curve, the railings and steps of its well-kept houses all on a
smaller scale than in Dublin. Nearby was a recruiting station
and the inevitable church.

Like any other tourist, Margaret began each day with an
early start, diligent in seeing the sights. On the walk along the
Mile, the first morning, the guide had the habit of repeating
what he had just said, not in different words, but the same.

As Senior Librarian her hostess, Heather, was invited to
official functions being held as part of the Festival. She

brought Margaret to the Lord Provost's Garden Party. The Queen's representative himself walked around among the bourgeoisie of Edinburgh wearing a chain.

A band of Sikhs played near them, drowning the crackling announcements over the public address system. No-one had told the band master (a regimental sergeant-major with magnificent whiskers) to keep the music low, and though people strained their ears irritably in the general direction of the organisers' tent, no-one seemed interested enough to take any action. Dancing feet that looked pointed, weaving in and out of pairs of crossed swords, brought only the very faintest spattering of polite applause.

It was the smell she noticed first. It was aromatic and racy, coming (she later learned) from a small nut he crushed between his teeth. Turning, she saw that the seat next to her had been taken by a short thickset Indian, quite distinguished-looking in a white raincoat and black umbrella but ill at ease as he tried, quickly (the play was about to begin) to stow them away without blocking the view of people sitting behind him.

"I am really very sorry," he said, more than once, as the seat banged upwards noisily.

At the interval he almost bumped against her as he came hurrying out of the Gents, and more profuse apologies followed. When *The Doctor and the Devils* ended she saw him, face gleaming with sweat, nerve himself to ask her: "What about coffee? Have you time?"

Why not? thought Margaret. Holidays were supposed to be like this, all casual meetings. At the top of the aisle she held his umbrella as he struggled with the white raincoat. She noticed it was a brand new Burbery, very stiff in the sleeves and shoulders, heavy for the mild dripping air of the night. In any case, now that she could see him full-length as it were, she sensed that the coat would work better if his broad shoulders were balanced by long legs and a confident gait.

The whole routine had to be gone through again in the overheated cafe where coffee hissed from an urn with a sharp release of steam. After he had wiped his glasses free of vapour the effort of holding his cup, scalding as if it were a newly sterilised hospital instrument, made him exude still more sweat.

After he had told her his name was Nassim and that he was Pakistani, they began to talk.

"Did you enjoy the play?" Margaret asked.

"Yes, well, course, my English, you know . . . I've so much to learn . . . " He looked down into the purplish-grey coffee and pulled off a piece of glistening doughnut.

"I found the Scottish accents a bit hard to follow, myself," she said, as she hoped, helpfully.

"I wouldn't be here at all only my boss suggested I should improve my education, and he passed on the tickets he had for tonight. He couldn't go himself. At the last moment, his wife got sick. I was lucky to return the other tickets to the box-office. I can just hear him teasing me when we're back in the office tomorrow about me not bringing a girl."

Margaret hadn't felt entitled to so detailed an account. Declining to respond in the same vein, she picked up something he had said. "Where do you go back to?"

"Glasgow. I work in the accounts department of a big company and my boss picked me to come with him here to Edinburgh to visit one of our client companies." He floundered, giggling, into an invitation for her to spend a weekend in Glasgow before she returned to Dublin.

"I myself have never seen Loch Lomond," he confided, "and I'll get tickets for the film *West Side Story*. It has just opened at the biggest cinema in Glasgow."

With only momentary hesitation, Margaret agreed, and before they parted outside the house in the Crescent, a rendezvous at the main railway station in Glasgow had been agreed on for the following Saturday noon. She felt that she should grab at anything that was offered. Just then, life was to be tackled, strenuously. It was so fascinating that she felt nothing could go wrong.

She told Heather that she was visiting a friend in Glasgow, and the suspicion she had had, that Heather would treat her as an equal, as another adult, proved well-founded.

She only said, "I'll see you on Sunday night, then, Margaret."

They met outside the station rather than, as arranged, inside. Nassim was still explaining and apologising for being late and for having necessitated her going to look for him, as they crossed a square fringed with large and hideous statues. On their bus journey through the city centre he pointed out cinemas and gave his opinion of each one. Finding him even more nervous than in Edinburgh, she enquired how his week had gone.

"My boss asked me all about the night at the theatre. He was surprised to hear that I enjoyed the play so much, and that I had met a girl from Dublin."

Margaret was beginning to take a silent aversion to his boss, when he nudged her broadly. They were passing the biggest cinema in town, and huge posters were advertising *West Side Story*. "I have tickets for this evening," he whispered.

At his lodgings in a dilapidated suburb far removed from the centre she met his compatriots, his friends: like him, book-keepers, watchful, deferential, given to nervous smiling and shrill giggles, but quite deficient in humour. In honour of her arrival, they had bought cans of beer.

"Margaret prefers wine," Nassim said proudly. It was perhaps the first time he had surprised, had come near to impressing them, and he called upon everything he knew about her as he bathed in the warm spring of his happiness.

They dreamed, Margaret thought, of being promoted at work (even if they remained over-qualified for their jobs), of being accepted as British (which meant English, rather than Scottish) and had to do with wearing raincoats, smoking pipes, buying the *Daily Express* and concealing all interest in, all knowledge of, their own origins. Beside them, she felt composed, blessed by fortune.

The reason for the visit to the lodgings had not been given, but Nassim's wish to show her off clearly partly accounted for it. Further, he meant to deposit her overnight bag there before they went off to the pictures. Persuaded that if she took the initiative he would be too shy to say anything, she picked up the bag after she had taken her leave of them all. She saw the eldest of them, the one who owned several houses let to young couples, noticing her gesture.

Nassim carried the bag on the bus and around the City Art Gallery where they spent an hour. "I'm going to come here more often in future," he commented as they ran from the Gallery steps to the bus.

Margaret's decisiveness over the business of the bag certainly stemmed in the first instance from the freedom to act that money confers. Her stay in Edinburgh having taken almost nothing from her savings, she had ample means to book a room in a plain but clean little hotel.

After the cinema, they had an Indian meal (at his insistence, accompanied by wine for Margaret). She tried to find out something about his home place.

"But do you not want to go back there someday?" She pressed him, delighted by the complex smells and tastes of the food in what was clearly a very average restaurant.

He conveyed a sense of hurt in his reply that was of a different nature from his usual bemused air. The question could simply not be considered. "All my friends are here," he said finally, but she knew he didn't regard that as the true reason.

On the poky landing of the hotel, he gripped her in his arms. She had never felt such need in anyone. It reflected something close to desperation, something stored in him for years. He was shaken as if by a tempest.

Their first view of the Loch wasn't very inviting: a broad path flanked by hut-like buildings purveying rolls of film and postcards led to jetties where small launches used for the pleasure-trips nestled. Beyond the bridge another path, exactly like the first, led in the opposite direction.

Though it was early for lunch, he stopped at once outside the most garish of the cafes. When it came to British eating-places, he seemed to be tempted into the overpriced and ill-run ones. In front was a self-service area where young hikers were feasting on buns and coca-cola. Margaret suggested that they stop in that part for a snack, but Nassim would have none of it.

"We must have a proper lunch. It's our last day, after all."

He might have felt a certain diffidence about sitting near a crowd, because of being with a white girl.

The main room was enormous, decorated with bilious pictures of the Loch and environs. From a menu shielded in clammy plastic they chose lamb, peas and chips. The first thing to arrive was a large pot of tea, which they had not ordered. He had been just on the point of going through the routine about what he called 'your wine' when the weary waitress had abruptly left them. Margaret was beginning to be bored with his little jokes about it. But this thick brown teapot, filled no doubt with thick brown tea, all at once became a challenge to him to assert himself.

Leaving such matters to the man — he paid the bill and it was he, after all, who had insisted on coming there — was part of the expected pattern. Slightly ironical, she asked: "Are you going to send the tea back?"

"Of course, but the girl has gone away now."

He somehow contrived to miss the opportunity when she arrived back, and as they pushed away plates on which the pale-coloured food was already stiffening into grease, the teapot was still in front of them.

The prospect of a trip by water compensated Margaret for the bored air of the ferryman as he took their tickets at the end of the jetty. The young hikers crowded into the bows of the boat, and she and Nassim moved towards the stern, as it took a southerly course.

After the animation of the previous night, they were both silent, each of them for a different reason. Hence the misery Margaret felt. The scenery chimed with her mood: she wanted the trip, the day, to be over. She longed to lay eyes again on the massive black buildings of Glasgow, even the sad suburban shops, instead of this endless green and brown.

What was she doing there anyway? Why had she come? She could have been listening in on arty chat at the Festival Club, or reading by Heather's congenial fireplace, a plate of

home-made bannocks nearby. She had been looking at herself, not Nassim, from the beginning. She felt sick, but not
because she was staring at the wake of the boat, not even
because of the leaden lunch. She was sick at her own vanity
and self-regard.

She would have to put a stop to the plan he was already
hatching, to take his Christmas holidays in Dublin. His boss
would notice that his elation was subdued and would ask
him about his Irish girlfriend. The mood of malice she had
yielded to in the episode of the teapot was altogether dissi-
pated. Now she could feel only sympathy for him.

And the attraction he had to Loch Lomond: had it been
kindled when he was in school? She began to imagine the English book they had used in the school in Karachi. It had
drawings and a few grainy photographs: London bobbies,
Beefeaters, the Boat Race, the Houses of Parliament, West-
minster Abbey, the Lake District and Loch Lomond. The
teacher, fervent in his faith that what he would never see
was well worth seeing, had urged his pupils to make excursions, if they got to Britain, to all those famous sights.

What was wrong with the Loch? Had too many postcards,
too many souvenirs robbed it of its reality? As in a way, the
teacher had robbed the pupils of their own lives. And what
she, Margaret, was doing to Nassim was somehow a part of
it all. She was so overwhelmed that she began to feel he
should never have left Pakistan, never come to take up a
British identity. She suddenly felt wildly maternal towards
him, anxious to spare him pain. If he stayed in Britain,
he would never get things right. He would always blame himself, not his boss, not his more successful friends, not the
rotten world. He would be robbed of his own life.

How paradoxical it was. She had first behaved in the way
she had understood to be right, guided by the twin principles
of retaining her biggest asset till the right man made the right
offer; and secondly she had enjoyed his admiration, exerted
charm, being as her mother put it 'squired' in the meantime.
Now, in recoil from her indifference to his scaldingly sincere
feelings, she was tempted, she also, to mediate the world

for him, to spare him pain. She realised bitterly that she could think of no atonement that was not a further insult.

The boat had by now completed its tour of the main stretch of the Loch, including the statutory approach close under one shore. The dew of evening was augmented by steady, weeping rain as it headed back towards the jetty from the north. On the sweep of drive in front of a pictur-esque castle that came briefly into view stood a tall narrow shape of bright yellow, some sort of oil tank, perhaps — at that distance she couldn't be sure, not that it mattered what it actually was. It contrasted with the scenery, with the famous attractions of the place: the romantic hills, rocks and trees, the castles with their gunmetal grey walls. For Margaret it was an attestation of life, of joy. Suddenly freed from her guilt about Nassim, she tuned into what he was saying. After the stock scenery talk, came the stock weather talk.

"I should have brought my mackintosh," he murmured. "My boss told me I'd get great value from it in Scotland."

"Was it he who suggested that you buy it?"

"Yes. He takes a great interest in me, in showing me the ropes as he says."

The moisture lay in unstable drops on his glossy black hair As if the colour had faded, the palms of his hands were a greyish buff colour, much lighter than the backs. He cradled her hand in both of his as they travelled in the bus back to Glasgow. She was so quiet that he joked.

"A penny for your thoughts. That's what my boss says when I start daydreaming in the canteen."

"Do you ever daydream at your desk?" she asked, curiosity having broken through her glum reverie.

"No, rarely, but maybe from now on, if I get a letter from someone special, I'll find it hard to keep my nose to the grindstone."

She pretended not to know what he meant, but his next remark could not be ignored.

"Is it permitted for me to write to your father?"

They were nearly into the Central Bus Station, and time

[92]

was short to pick up her bag and catch the last Sunday train to Edinburgh.

"Look, Nassim, I don't want to get serious about anyone just now. I have to finish my degree, earn some money and travel."

"Of course, I can wait," he insisted, "I want you to have a good time. But your father and I ought to reach an understanding."

Telling fibs offered no way out. Time, or her future plans had nothing essential to do with the matter, as she well knew. So she began to explain, hoping that he would twig quickly, so that she wouldn't have to spell it out and bruise him still more.

She got on the train with the job more than half done.

Five students sat in the narrow pew-like benches of a room that was somewhat unfrequented and consequently had a neglected air. It matched somehow the gaunt face of the tutor, his pale nervous fingers and the way he twisted one leg around the other so that one grey-socked and black-shod foot stuck, twitching, into the air. He sat at a desk on a little square podium which rose only four inches or so from the floor.

The first text they had to read was *The Duchess of Malfi*. Margaret had been attracted by the brevity and passion of the play, and she volunteered to comment. "The villain, Bordello, reminded me of Richard the Third, taking the role of the malcontent."

She felt satisfied to have made such a connection, to have acquired a vocabulary that allowed her to toss off terms like 'malcontent'. But she began to realise that the tutor was laughing at her mispronunciation of the character's name. Smiling thinly, he murmured: "I'd explain if you were older."

She had been aware that the mistake had a certain appropriateness, that one could talk of Freudian slips. But why had Mr Hennessy not simply pronounced it correctly, to cue

[93]

her, or laughed with her about it? She was dismayed that a lecturer in college could turn out so much like a sarcastic teacher at school, exploiting vulnerability for his own fleeting success, putting a brake on her enthusiasm, disabling discourse. She had so many reasons for touchiness: being young, being female, being ambitious, being shy. How could she guess that it was her own touchiness that made him react that way? She remained guarded, loath to take chances in his class again.

The discussion went from one student to the tutor, never between students, though with the small number, they came to know each other pretty well. He was not a popular tutor. He came late (when he came at all) and generally looked disagreeable. When he failed to show up they did not proceed with a tutorial among themselves, but grinned ruefully at each other and repaired to the steamy annexe for coffee that seemed to partake of the quality of the cream wall, the pale green woodwork, the brown lino.

Secretly, Margaret preferred this outcome: there were worse things than crossing the Main Hall in the company of three males, two at least of them college characters, Dramsoc members, whose progress over the black and white tiles would normally be punctuated only by the salutes of other characters, who were known by sight to many who would not have dared to salute them.

The eldest, Peadar O'Keefe, looked like St John of the Cross. He had, apparently, only just left a seminary in England. His jaws were lean and bluish, his body angular, and he wore dark coloured clothes that looked one size too small. He never said anything remarkable, but somehow one always expected just that of him.

Gerald Carmody was a Jesuit student. His chunky figure, his horn-rimmed glasses, his gold cufflinks pinching starched linen, as well as his rounded tones, exuded confidence. He was always well prepared and discussed the texts with confidence, neatening his book of notes as he presented a point.

Peter was an American. His acquaintance with the tutor originated outside of college, in the Leeson Street bar that was the resort of medical students, with the old half deaf professor of anatomy at the centre of the talk. Peter wore Madras cotton jackets and white trousers. He smoked and drank more than the constitutions, let alone the pockets, of most other first years allowed. For most of his career in college he was promising to speak on Nietzsche to the Philosophical Society. The long-promised paper was finally delivered in the third term of their final year. Though Nietzsche was much in vogue he was not on the course; the attendance was therefore poor. At that point in the year most students were nailed to their books and notes in the library. Those who attended the lecture found it disappointing, bearing the signs of hasty preparation and superficial reading, thinly spread. Peter's reputation had been bound up with the success of the paper, but his scamped performance did not diminish it. Margaret had by then come to realise that most people in college surpassed her above all only in what was most vital: the cheek, the presumption to put themselves forward.

Even after Margaret had started college and was aiming at an academic career, Dutch prayed hard that she would meet someone nice. When Margaret was awarded a scholarship for study in America, Dutch felt disappointed that she seemed to be distancing herself from taking up a nice career like a hostess at the airport. Working in Collinstown would have put Margaret more in the way of meeting someone nice, of getting married in her early twenties. Businessmen, professional men, foreigners, travelled by plane. She often feared that Margaret risked putting off someone nice by sounding too clever or by having unusual views on things. Men, after all, did not marry girls like that: they married girls who relied on them to set their wives right about politics, sport or world affairs, to give them money for clothes and make-up, to keep out of their way in the kitchen, and not to object if the wives wanted to go on doing modelling or secretarial work part-time.

Men had the biggest say in things, but they had, Dutch thought, to be overruled in the domestic world. They lacked foresight about practical matters, but this could be conceded to them, as could their missing Mass by lying in bed on Sunday mornings, staying late in town with friends who were (or behaved as if they were) bachelors. They were often coarse, their breath and eyes full of whiskey, with tobacco coughs and a tendency to urinate, spit or vomit in back lanes at night. Especially on Friday evenings, when Mooney's of Earl Street had been full from five o'clock on, the lane outside the garment showrooms where Dutch worked would be in a disgusting state.

They could be guilty of other public spillages, too, like the man who had come from behind her at the counter in Woolworth's and had pushed into her free hand (the other was holding a jar of Pond's Cold Cream at the time) a hard swollen penis. Stunned, she brought her face around without, at first, releasing her hand and saw, in the throng of faces, a small dapper man.

Margaret was hoping that she'd run into lots of fellow-students on their way to lunch in 86, as she dashed, dozens of times, from the Little Theatre to the Aula, wearing her woman of Argos costume from *The Flies*. At the rate the dress rehearsal was going, her little scene near the beginning of Act II would not be played till evening. But the cast had an unspoken pact to stay and help fetch stuff or finish the daubing of the statue's face with red paint that represented blood. None of them had been near a lecture, or the library, for days.

She liked being seen in the costume because it proclaimed her membership of a select band, dedicated to each other and to the show. Never had she shared as much with others as now with the theatricals. They were all in the know about life, imbued with the exhilaratingly bleak philosophy of the play. Peter spoke about freedom beginning on the far side of despair, about the end of the reign of the gods.

She tiptoed to where Peter, who was directing, sat astride a chair.

"Oh, Jesus, Paddy's accent is pure Falls Road sometimes," he announced in a whisper as, accompanied by Peadar O'Keefe in the role of his Voltairean tutor, the male lead found his way into the town that was sunk in guilt and sunlight.

"Still, his legs look great."

They had all whistled and clapped the first time Paddy had appeared as Orestes with his legs coated in brown make-up, holding his sturdy blunt profile at the best angle, keeping his sword free from entanglement in the cloak. It was intended to make up for all the shortcomings of the rest of the costume and give him a fine swirl on his exits.

In the first enthusiastic meetings that had preceded their choice of the play for the Universities Drama Festival, Margaret and the others had been persuaded that Peter knew a lot about Sartre and the Existentialists, and even more about staging plays. Both beliefs had by now dimmed, but with what they fancied was the appropriate defiant spirit they stuck with the show. Peter might not be, as he had first suggested, a genius who could work in any field of art and had chosen the theatre, but he had unquestionably been inspired in the matter of the set. He had found a photo of a production in Warsaw for which the designer had made an Expressionist bunker of the Temple of Apollo, capturing the spirit of Occupied Europe where the expression of the will to assert freedom had to be clandestine. The human consciousness was radically free — no excuses were permissable — and that privity buoyed them up, gave them a swagger of superiority over their classmates.

Feelings of this sort, intense yet vague, were channelled as much by the Edith Piaf LP as by *The Flies*, and playing the record repeatedly during rehearsals had been Peter's idea and the second good thing he had done.

It gave them what they needed: the chance to experience new kinds of unhappiness. What they had sensed of Occupation sadness and betrayal, of Liberation courage and emotionality, seduced them. Life was, surely, unsafe: it might be as stagey as the songs that Piaf belted out, but it was never dull, never the sleepy business they imagined it was for their parents, their teachers, whom they would never resemble.

Not bringing the set up North for the tryout before the Festival might have been their undoing, reducing the impact of the production. The jaunt had started well enough, though: to their satisfaction, some of the girls from Dominican Hall were around the Green when they set off, early one Sunday, and asked surprisedly where they were going in the very large tour bus that stood outside 86.

The Trinity crowd who had asked to come were, it transpired, only three in number. They had an enviable style, especially the girl. She wore jeans and chain-smoked. Despite being outnumbered, they were a forceful presence on the bus, singing verse after verse of a song that seemed daring, because the chorus went:

"When the red revolution comes.
We'll make old Winston Churchill
Smoke a Woodbine cigarette
When the red revolution comes.
We'll make old de Valera
Sing the 'Sash Me Father Wore'
When the red revolution comes."

The fact of crossing the Border elicited from the UCD crowd a rather uncertain chorus of 'Kevin Barry'.

"Lads like Barry will free Ireland,
For her sake they'll live and die."

His picture was in the stained glass window of the room that had been the History Library: dressed not as a member of the Belvedere rugby team, but as Robert Emmet. They sang because they had to keep their end up in the face of the Trinity performance. They sang that song because it was

[98]

expected, it allowed them an air of indignation, of strong feelings that came automatically with little need to think: the words did it all.

"British soldiers tortured Barry . . .
Turn informer or we'll kill you . . .
Calmly standing to attention."

He had been like them, a middle-class student, not a labourer from West Cork or a clerk from Rathmines. The insidious power of song, even when as at that moment the songs were unequally matched, to make one feel enfolded and vulnerable at once, had prevailed.

Attempts were made to get other songs going, but neither the number one hit of the lately-dead Buddy Holly, nor 'My Darling Clementine' could take fire, could unite the two groups in chorus. With 'The Red Revolution' and 'Kevin Barry' they had shown their colours: not, certainly, their true colours, but the colours of their myths. In myth, one lot were iconoclastic, liberal-lefty, concerned with a whimsical view of the future, the other militantly nationalistic and anti-partitionist, concerned with a romantic view of the past.

Newry was dreadfully empty and poor. They did badly with the show, as it was played too fast and the atmosphere never really came alive. After the adjudicator had lectured them on the failings of the production they returned to Dublin, feeling tired, tight and incompetent. They could not find any way into the darkened and empty 86, but the lighting specialist, an engineer with a pioneer pin, edged on his toes across the ledge running around the area and found an open window. They parted with their accustomed salute: 'god bless, love', still feeling they had everything in common.

The female students' cloakroom where lockerless girls had to change in the toilet and store their bags in (they hoped) unnoticed corners, was large, drably painted in grey and reached by a staircase that also led to the nuns' cloakroom next door. It was rumoured that there were no mirrors on the nuns' walls, but not even the cheekiest would have dared to go in and check.

Margaret often thought of the nuns gathering up handfuls of black serge, heavy with beads, medals and the ends of their belts, to reach what were probably long, serviceable elasticated bloomers. As often as possible the nuns left the premises by the side door near their cloakroom. On wet days it was at this door that they crowded into the long black chauffeur-driven limousines that (by order, it was rumoured, of the Archbishop) conveyed them back to their convents.

Using the side door also released the nuns from the complications of crossing the flags of the Main Hall. On this dangerous, exciting expanse one longed to reach the stage — which came for some rapidly, for some never — of knowing sufficient of the boys who stretched themselves on the red plush benches to stop and chat or even to join them, though few were the audacious girls who went so far.

As they studied in the Library, the approach of the clock hands to twelve was invariably first noticed by a nun. After she had risen quietly to her feet, making a deep genuflection as if the table before which she stood had been an altar, most other students, in twos and threes, would follow. The only students that definitely never said the Angelus in this public way were not the few supposedly hardened atheists but the Jesuit clerics. They came across as more men of the world than even the law students, and sartorially were vastly different from the black-hatted, shambling Clonliffe lads who formed a mass as closely combined as the nuns.

Limited to taking Pass degrees and only in certain subjects, usually civil servants or teachers, the night students arrived on bicycles from their digs or bedsitters in the South or North Circular Road. Instead of 'College' they spoke of 'the Uni'. They knew little of the complex intrigues of the Main Hall, of society teas and L and H meetings. But they often went to dances in 86, and it was at one of these that Margaret met Padraig. She noticed his well-scrubbed hands and the fact that the cuffs of his white shirt did not show under the sleeves of his dark grey suit. She learned afterwards that he rolled up his shirt-cuffs to keep them clean for work a few days longer. As they danced, the hand that held hers passed a tremor from the thumb.

Looking at him coming back across the floor with minerals for them both, she saw a tall, bony young man whose hair waved back from his forehead in crinkly rows. He always looked a bit windblown: possibly it was his style or his origin among the glens of Donegal. Having a job in Customs and Excise meant that he could organise a taxi home for Margaret. In the back seat, he put his damp shaking hand on hers. He paid the taxi off at the gate of her house and on the step pulled her close and kissed her.

Feeling the row of biros that lined his inside jacket, she shifted more to the other side. She indicated her mother's lighted window and ran quickly up the steps, having arranged to meet him at the Theatre Royal the following Sunday night at eight.

During his lunch-hour Padraig had hurried over to Hawkins Street for the tickets. When the lights went down he began to rub the back of her hand with his thumb, his arm lying around her shoulder.

The little Lancashire man was perched aloft a huge strangely-lit organ which rose slowly from the space beside the stage. From its complex keyboard he extracted a medley of tunes (some of the day, but most much older) which emerged in gasps and runs, each lasting long enough to arouse a transient memory in the middle-aged couples who sat stiffly upright and smiling, or laughed heartily at the comic.

The Royalettes swung their shakoed heads stiffly in unison. So snappy was the precision of their joint movements that they seemed a creature possessed of twenty-four legs ending in white clog-like shoes, twenty-four interlocked arms ending in white gloves, the military motif echoed in the white silver-buckled belts holding in mauve sleeveless tunics over fishnet tights. Then followed singers, dancers, ventriloquists, with changes of lights, with music, breezy or defiant. Waves of applause broke over the white up-turned faces, like petals in the blackness.

Afterwards, in a pub frequented by ballad singers, one of his favourites, she asked him why he had suggested the Royal.

"You get a picture and a stage-show, it's better value." It was the argument that had led him to take girls there when first he came to Dublin.

"Maybe, but the pictures are really corny."

He was alert to pick up hints about what would please Margaret better, so that he began to suggest instead English films at the Metropole, later French and Italian films at the Astor, and finally plays at the Gate. Over the winter they went around together, the pattern changed. He began to stay in town after work and meet her in a pub where they sometimes stayed so late that the visit to the cinema was postponed or cancelled altogether. He once asked her to have tea in his flat, and she arrived at six. The kitchen had a functional iron cooker, a rickety worktop with cupboards underneath, the doors of which always stuck, and a formica-topped table, chipped at the edges.

Margaret went out with him for the evening's shopping: sliced pan, tomatoes in a flimsy bag, chops, rashers and eggs. He liked sweets, so he added mince slices and cream buns from under a plastic dome on the counter. All this came from a crowded little shop along the street.

A wedge of hardened grease, left over from breakfast, lay in the bumpy frying-pan. Padraig started to heat it up. As it melted, it provided a kind of soul of cooking medium to which the rashers, chops and sausages added their quota of fat. The eggs were cooked last. They were speckled with black. "I'll give the egg a miss, thanks," she said.

As they were eating, Padraig's flatmate, Eamonn, came in. Margaret thought that he had a cuter eye than Padraig, more calculating, better able to (as he would have said himself) suss out a situation. A primary school teacher in Ballyfermot, he was hoping finally to pass his BA that June. The month after, he was to marry a girl from Transport and

Power. The reception would take place at a hotel in Howth.

The flat had curtains that were skimpy: an autumn leaves pattern was just discernible under the dust that covered them, and the mustard-coloured nylon carpet was greasy in places. The record-player in the corner, like the empty pint Guinness bottles under the sink, dated from the last party, when they had played the Clancy Brothers and what Padraig called 'off-colour ballads'. The only personal things in the room were books: *Poems* of James Stephens, O'Casey's *Autobiographies*; and Padraig had, he said, a chance of borrowing the *Kama Sutra* from a fellow in work, as soon as three others had had their turn.

In honour of their date, he broke out a clean shirt from a cellophane laundry packet. He came back into the room, pulling on a sweater of a different colour but the same style as the cable-stitch turquoise one he had been wearing. Both were, she knew, the work of his sister at home.

Seeing Margaret look around the flat, Eamonn asked ingratiatingly: "It's filthy, like our minds, isn't it?", as if sure of her approval.

"The girlfriend gives it a bit of a going-over now and then. Maybe you'd like to give her a hand the next time?"

Margaret was aware of Padraig's anxious face as he waited for her reply, afraid that it would be cutting. He understood that Eamonn's way of talking failed completely to fit the way they were together. Nor would he ever think that the flat needed much looking after: he spent time and money rather on books or in pubs.

Padraig had, at different times, hoped to rise from the Customs Section to the Department of Finance, or that his exam results would justify his embarking on an MA course. When these hopes finally evaporated he settled, with a tinge of the mild cynicism that was becoming his habitual frame of mind, to his well-paid, unspectacular job, his visits to pubs, and to Margaret. With much free time and an office that was virtually private, he could ring her up often for a date, for a chat.

As Margaret left College one balmy afternoon, a tar machine was in action just down from the gate. From the rear of the puffing engine a large pancake of tar dropped, to be rolled out thin and flat at the edge of the roadway. The tang of tar was in the air and Margaret was light-hearted as she crossed into the Green, which was dappled with sunlight. Past the group of the Three Fates in bronze, she met Gerald Carmody. Their common membership of Mr. Hennessy's tutorial provided them with an excuse to stop. She noticed the unfamiliar characters in the book Gerald was supporting on his neat, black, zipped briefcase, making of it a portable lectern.

"What's that you're studying?" she asked.

He held up the cover, in brooding black and red. The *Penguin Russian Course*.

"But in Stephen's Green?"

"I never waste any time," he beamed. "Since the beginning of the year I've progressed as far as Lesson 6. Not bad for peripatetic study a few minutes a day, is it?"

Not bad at all, she agreed, wondering what peripatetic meant, tempted to ask him why he and his confrere (a regular attender at the Film Society, versed in Fellini, Bergman and Bresson) never rose to say the Angelus in the library.

He invited her to hear a paper being read at Hatch Hall the next night on the conflict between Christianity and Communism. "Afterwards there'll be an informal party in Mills'," he explained.

"They're spreading tar near the College gates," she told him confidingly. "In this country we must use the most antique kind of tar-making machine in the world. It's really terrific."

He turned for Lower Leeson Street, even on that warm day a frosty place, while Margaret continued on past the bull-rushes at the centre of a dry fountain. They were now more of a treasure than ever, since they had been newly painted a pale glistening brown. They bristled from a cluster of metal leaves, firm-set phallic shapes, each one finished with a tiny nib — doubtlessly made at a time when it was considered proper to cover the legs of pianos.

Margaret hung her head down over the edge of the low divan. Padraig's black winter-cracked Clery's shoe lay beside her face. It was the strangest thing she had ever seen, and it led her to consider the strangeness of Padraig himself. After long scrutiny of the shoe, she turned to look at him, very close to her in the narrow bed. He had taken his shoes off quite early on in the night, along with his jacket, his tie and his shawl-collared sweater. The memory of how he had looked when, later, he had crossed the room to put out the light, his underpants slack and baggy above stringy legs, slipped back. It was surprising. He was usually particularly modest, going outside even to change his shirt. He must have been quite drunk. And she?

A few nights before, Eamonn had taken his Mairead off on honeymoon to Majorca. The turbulence of that event had left Padraig queasy: he seemed restless, a bit nervous even, in the pub and on the way back to the flat with some of his friends. Margaret's plan was to take a taxi home, but she found herself very sleepy, stretched out on the blanket-covered divan. Padraig lay beside her, next to the wall. He tested her breasts through the jumper and she sensed the haste, the unhandiness of his gestures. There were really too many clothes around, she reflected, as he pushed up her skirt and kicked his trousers into a bundle at the end of the bed. It must have been some time later that she had seen him going across to the light-switch by the door and that she had slipped under a single blanket, keeping away from the stale, tousled sheets. Then he had pulled down his underpants and it had occurred to her that his heavy socks were still on: the thought was altogether unappealing. But that had been by no means the only or the most cramping aspect of the attempted seduction. Padraig, whether by Guinness or diffidence, had been quite undone.

She mused on his length, his vulnerability to her gaze. He twitched occasionally, spasms tightening his belly. The warmth, the disorder of his sleeping body was revealed to her, closed in on itself, yet also unguardedly open. Odd curls of hair grew on his pale chest, and the shoulders were scattered with freckles. She lifted the blanket.

One leg was bent under him, so that two lines ran together in a V, the split of his buttocks and the deep crease joining it. At that point there was a dark blur of hair deepening into where a slack, wrinkled red pouch hung down. How did it feel to have that kind of packet, so complex, so old-looking, in one's trousers?

"I'll be very careful", he had assured her the night before. "I'll come out in time." The hoped-for erection, penetration, had not taken place: she knew that it should not be that way, still a little wrinkled handful, too much skin for the knobbly lumps inside. Breathing hard, he had tried again and again, till he dropped into sleep just before she did.

He started to explain at breakfast, when she was off to lectures and he to the office. "I had too many pints last night, I'm sorry."

"You never have to say that to me." She meant it, but he couldn't believe her.

Artlessly, he went on, about how he often got sick, down home, over the breakfast fry brought to him by his mother. He was going to cut it out altogether. He had tried the other, without drink taken, but he was terribly nervous. When, eventually, he had dared to mention it, the doctor had not even suggested an examination, had told him it would be all right when he got married. "You'll be the makings of me, pet," he smiled confidingly at Margaret, thinking also of the rented apartamento, of Eamonn and his presumed potency, and of Mairead. The jokes of his friends at the wedding had lamented "another decent man gone" and designated him as the next.

Margaret understood: he had behaved as if everything was settled for them to marry but, seeing her as the more decisive, the more enterprising, with more scope for changes in her life, he almost seemed to leave it to her to suggest when they got engaged or married. He had not thought of checking on her feelings and, up to then, neither had she.

For the rest of the day she grappled with the conundrum: if only he hadn't told her his secret. It brought up the question of marriage in a more urgent form.

In its way, the admission had been a proposal: she was now implicated, held responsible for helping him to a cure. She found that nothing could have appealed to her less than to marry anyone and set up house in Terenure, minding first wedding presents and then babies. Padraig would come home late sometimes with men friends. She thought she already knew what that would be like: his sheepish look, his arm around her shoulders, the bag of Guinness bottles. In his soft way, he had the ability to dissipate her anger, and she feared that more than anything, because the source of her anger would remain unrevealed.

It was so easy and pleasant, their life, at least until the previous night's difficulty, that very little more would have been sufficient to draw them into marriage. Margaret saw that state as the people around her saw it: the inevitable, the fit conclusion to a woman's growing-up, involving bills and rows but also the attainment of a place in society. If she were to acquire a husband with a steady job, a nice house and, in due course, a given number of babies, it would re-assure everyone. She was, after all, fitting in, opting to hand over to a man the responsibility for keeping her, for dealing with important matters for her.

There were many examples of the apparently natural pro-gression. When she met Niamh from school, just returned from the Continent, she heard all about Niamh's fiance of a few weeks: Declan had a great future in gynae. Suzanne was marrying Fergus, who would quickly progress to a partnership in the solicitors' firm founded by his uncle. Many of her classmates in College had done their Finals with new engagement rings flashing on their fingers, arousing gallant or paternal responses in the middle-aged professors of Italian, Social Science or Physiotherapy. Of these friends Margaret felt a fleeting — a very fleeting — envy, for their freedom from the confusions that seemed in her case to multiply, just when they could have been expected to

[107]

dwindle.

Yet she continued to trust her stubborn feeling that the pattern would not work for her. That led to a consideration of Padraig. She had finished by playing games with him and now, especially, she had to desist. His niceness, his companionship, had captured her in a way that she had let him misunderstand.

When at last the break came, she was shattered by the effect it had on him. Shaken out of his placidity, tears forced from his eyes, he dealt briskly with her for the first time in her experience. His distress so marked him that she was almost scared. The hurt buried deep had shown through and set him apart. He was suddenly powerful: he cut short her rationalisations and headed out of the door. She had cruelly cheated him by being so prodigal of her own enjoyment of life. Though he should of course have asked her, she should of course have told him, how things lay.

The open-plan house in County Galway was full of low tables with books: *The Rise and Fall of the Third Reich, The Marsh Arabs*. It had also new stereo equipment and woven rugs. The curtains were of stone-coloured wool. Through the wedged crowds in the drawing-room the small donkey pushed his way. Though the house had been built for some time, the grounds (they could not be described as a garden) had not yet been tamed or shaped. The grass was intermittent, coarse and tufty. Out-croppings of rock were everywhere bewildering. The donkey had, presumably, been introduced by Dan O'Shaughnessy, a middle-aged American in a bawneen jacket, to give a flavour of Connemara to his party. The guests were students taking part in the Drama Festival at Galway that Easter, a sample of the party-going population of Pembroke Road and Fitzwilliam Square. They drank Guinness out of fine china cups, pint bottles, champagne glasses and pewter mugs. The donkey was offered a saucerful, but he only sniffed it. In the background was playing the record that belonged to a set with the Third

Reich book. Everyone subsided by degrees to the floor or the skirting: women with their legs stretched out, men squatting on their heels.

The sounds of one of Hitler's early addresses at Nuremberg grew fainter as Margaret moved towards the toilet. When she reached it, she saw that the door was open. Sue, one of the Trinity crowd, had passed out after dropping ash into her drink. Friends held her, one on each side, as she leaned, retching and shaking, over the bowl. Downstairs, Sue took one sip of the tepid black instant coffee that they pressed on her and left, to be taken back to her digs in Galway. All those who had seen her up close were more shaken than they pretended. Margaret moved around, chatting: she heard people impressing those who had not realised what was happening by knowledgeable-sounding hints about the effects of various mickey finns.

"Coca-cola and aspirin, that's really wild."

"A fellow in our class took benzedrine the night before his Finals and was sure he'd got on great on the first two papers. But all he'd done was to write his name over and over again, up and down the sides of the paper."

"A good *poitín* — you don't know what you've been missing till you try it."

The Horst Wessel Lied was thumping over the two speakers. Finding that she didn't want to hear it so loudly, Margaret moved towards the mantelpiece, from which she would have a good view round the room.

From where she stood, beside the mantelpiece, he was staring at her, and she stared back, liking everything about him: his small close-knit figure, his artfully chopped blonde hair, his pliant hands.

"Do you know what my favourite quotation from Blake is?" he asked her.

"No, but I'd love to hear."

"The road of excess leads to the palace of wisdom."

She laughed as he went on: "Will you have a drink with me?"

On their way back from the kitchen, they paused in the

dark hall. Margaret beckoned him to look out of the window.

On the grass, frosted with moonlight, O'Shaughnessy's Irish Wolfhound was playing alone. He sniffed the breeze that tossed his abundant coat. He sprang onto the rocks, he scraped at the ground, he stretched out his neck and tail, and stood quite still for one moment, as if lost in a dream, a ceremony. They felt separated, not only by the difference in species, but as if by centuries and by the mystery that had fallen upon him, as he strode, majestic and playful, through the world that for the moment belonged to him.

It seemed natural for Christopher to take Margaret's hand as they watched from the window, the opening for them onto a world nobly indifferent to their concerns. They could not share in such sorcery, but the inductance of the dog's energy pulled them from the weaker field of the party: first to the stairs, where Margaret sat enfolded in the fork of his legs, and later to the first adjacent bedroom. There, in secret jubilation, they closed, combined. The stir of his body, the way it saluted her presence, opened in Margaret a juicy tunnel as softly lustrous as the cavity of an oyster.

Downstairs, the racket declined into drowsy argument or listless seduction. Outside, the moonlight was still strangely shed. She started to laugh, almost choking on the Player's Number One (the last of her packet) that he was putting into her mouth.

"I can't think why I started to talk to you: I usually can't stand people who keep their coats around their shoulders at parties. It looks affected: as if they've somewhere better to go."

"Well, if you won't say why, I'll have to, won't I? I'm quite simply irresistible."

Her head was in his lap as he sat on the floor, the duffle coat she had spoken of still draped around his shoulders.

They pretended for a while not to notice the first signs of day that were edging the closed blinds. The night — it was mid-April, after all — had been too short: all too soon, the dawn came, watery and chill.

The kitchen was beginning to draw rumpled figures from

all parts of the house. Coffee, tea, toast from a six-slice toaster, went around with the last of the cigarettes. Margaret sat on one of Christopher's knees. She rejoiced in the hardness of his thigh: muscle tightening under her buttocks. He was of only average height, but the rowing that he did at Trinity had made him very strong: she liked that. As they held their mugs of coffee, she put her free arm around his shoulder and he put his free arm around her waist. A pale golden blur of stubble had come out on his face.

They introduced each other to their friends, spontaneous, carefree, eager to show, to proclaim, their happiness.

Curious to see the effects of such a long vigil on her features, Margaret faced the wide mirror over the mantelpiece. From the corner came a voice she didn't recognise.

"Are you putting on a full layer of fresh make-up?"

The question made her start laughing again, but in sheer friendliness for the girl who had spoken and whom she didn't even see properly. Hardly had she caught an impression of a large well-kept bouffant hairdo when Chrisopher, coming up beside her, cupped her eyes with his hands as he kissed her.

"It was here, to the strains of the Horst Wessel Lied, that we met: how long ago it seems," he whispered. "Let's grab our places in Geoffrey's car and get back to Galway."

"Should we thank O'Shaughnessy before we go?" she asked.

"I think he'll survive without seeing us. In fact, remembering how lovely his girlfriend is, I'm sure he will."

Outside, as they made their way towards a Ford Consul that seemed to have about twelve people squeezed in already, he slung his coat around Margaret's shoulders.

"This is why I've been holding on to it."

She rubbed the close-woven fawn wool with her cheek. They piled into the car. The driver, a swarthy young man, was fending off the bitter protests of stragglers left behind.

"It's fourteen miles to Galway, you know."

"No problem," said the swarthy young man. "Plenty of people around before long, going to Mass. It's Sunday, you understand. You'll easily hitch a lift once you're on the main road."

"What about all the sex maniacs around? The country's full of them," a girl challenged him.

"Really? I congratulate you on your luck."

Geoffrey swung the car around in a circle towards Galway. As yet no feeling of day, or any heat, had crept into the air. After the debauchery of having been awake all night, to go to Mass in the Franciscan Church seemed to Margaret and Christopher a fitting sequel. They stood at the back of the church, as Mass had already started, and pointedly did not approach the altar at the Communion with the rest of the congregation. At this hour it consisted mainly of women and children, but counted also some elderly men and Guards who held their caps under their arms.

Standing among them, with his coat still around her shoulders, Margaret felt that she partook of their thanks, their praise, of all the thanks and praise that were hallowing the morning. She was buoyed up by the discoveries born of the night that had just finished, the talk that left her hunger to know all about Christopher still unsatisfied, by the journey through the magical, awakening countryside, going at that moment through the first of the changes (of light, of visage) that would follow in the course of the day. Now the unpretentious devotion of this company of docile believers, the undistinguished church with its mass-produced ikons, copies of earlier Italian works, seemed the harbingers of a new life, adventurous, all-demanding.

In one of the few cafes open so early in the season on Sunday she talked to Christopher. They wondered why Mass had come so naturally, as they were both quite undutiful Catholics.

"I think I wanted to sort of dedicate myself . . . it's hard to explain."

He nodded. "I know what you mean. I've never felt like this before. I never thought one could feel like this." Then, in a lighter key, he went on: "In my family, it's one of the issues my parents have been tussling about, whether I should be sent to Catholic schools."

"What did they decide?"

"I've changed schools so often, we were always moving house — some of the schools were Catholic, some not. Since they got divorced, I notice my father is more devout — he's the Catholic one, my mother is non-practising C. of E. — and he's always hoping to hear that I've returned to the fold. Wait till I tell him about you: he's Irish himself, and he thinks the Irish are smashing."

"It must have been tough on you when they broke up."

"Not as tough as knowing that I was the reason they were staying together, till I was eighteen and out of school."

She guessed that some kind of strain, besides the marital disagreements, accounted for the frequent moves, the changes of school, the holidays spent with half-familiar grandparents and aunts.

The first time they went out in Dublin, she met him at the front gate. Her lover, her friend, her brother: he was really there. They lay against the railings for a few minutes before moving off into the town, into the evening splendid with promise. They headed out of the softly-glowing street into the Paradiso, where the walls were decorated with improbable-looking desert island scenes in loud greens and oranges, the stairs hung with signed portraits of stars of stage and radio, who had eaten there, as they claimed, unforgettably: Gracie Fields, Fred Astaire, Benny Goodman.

As they breathed in the scent of grilled steak and mushrooms, Christopher joked: "Study the menu and order a coffee."

Laughing at him, letting her knee touch his under the table, she did. She would have liked to do more: in that public place, she would have liked to cast off her shoe, and put her foot up under the table, to feel which side of his well-cut crotch it was on, the little prominence.

They could sit on and on over a single cup of coffee and it was the kind of night he enjoyed, cheap and full of talk. Afterwards, they would take the bus or a slow intimate walk back to her house, and have more coffee, sometimes with her mother.

They did not always go to the Paradiso, though it always remained a happy, a lucky place. At weekends they went to boat races at Islandbridge, and to a party afterwards laid on by the committee. Other evenings he signed her in as a visitor to his rooms, and they would sit on the lumpy sofa as the long summer evening waned and the time to bring her home approached.

He mentioned a possible visit by his father to Dublin, but nothing came of it. Their terms were close to ending: for Margaret, the last one; her Finals were in September. They were proud of being disciplined, of giving up nights, she to study, he to rowing practice. She sometimes found him cramped for funds: she fancied that he was trying to get as far as he could in Trinity society without the means that others could rely on. He always smoked her cigarettes and once asked her for a loan of money.

"I think you're bit of a social climber," she said to him once, and she noticed how he covered up with laughter the slight start that escaped him.

"Of course I am, my darling: I'm trying for a career in the Foreign Office, and you need more than a First in History for that." Another time, they planned how best he could spend the summer.

"Once I see you settled into study and a hermit's life I'll find a job in an office in London, so that I can pay back some of my creditors."

"I hope that includes me," she said, "though I'd rather have you here to hold my hand."

"I promise to ring you up every second morning, so you'd better not go to the library till after lunch."

She became a connoisseur of libraries: adept at securing places under the green-shaded lamps of the National Library, sometimes using the reader's ticket he had fixed up for her for Trinity, so as to recapture a little of his ambience, to run into his friends: of course, she also needed to keep in touch with her class by going to UCD.

They had agreed not to go out with anyone else. Margaret

worked diligently, early and late. She was solaced: at home by cups of coffee, by cheese and onion sandwiches that her mother made and that Mary brought up to her bedroom: in the libraries by quick cigarettes on the steps, by ritual laments about how little work everybody was doing, and especially by his phone calls. Ringing always from the office of the big store where he worked, he brought her a ration, a portion of joy that sustained her till the next morning.

Her happiness and sense of purpose in life made her much more visible, more in demand with boys than formerly, but she stuck to their agreement.

She met him off the boat train on his return in early September, and they hurried to his rooms to catch up on the news. He had, she thought, acquired a more polished manner from his sojourn in London. The following week her exams began, and she rang him up each evening to report on the trials of the day. When the results came out she was proud, not only of her success in getting a First, but of having him there at the notice board, showing so much aplomb as he mixed with her classmates. That special night they went out to a pub.

In the crowded weeks that followed, Margaret had many decisions to make. She accepted an offer to work as a tutor in College and go on to an MA.

Christopher had a new room-mate that year, and he spoke often of Nigel and how Margaret must meet him. He was planning to cut down on rowing as his own Finals loomed nearer. She could not escape an insidious sense of disappointment. She had never found him again after the London trip: he was, if anything, more attentive but the ease, the newness they had known with each other was damaged: hard to say how, exactly, but equally hard not to sense that it had been damaged.

The weekend after her results came out, Nigel invited them to go for a drive and back to a party in Trinity. They stopped outside Switzer's in the car while Nigel went in to collect the last member of the party, a London beauty consultant called Diana, who was that month demonstrating the products of her firm in the store. They moved off along Nassau Street. While they waited at traffic lights, Nigel noticed a girl who, like many others that bright day was strolling to meet her boyfriend.

"She's very pretty."

"Yes, dear, but they're all the same when you get close — always a bit coarse, the Irish, don't you think?" drawled Diana. The uncomfortable silence that followed informed her that she had said something wrong.

"Oh, is Margaret . . . ."

Margaret found the whole episode difficult to shrug off during the rest of the day and it remained a slight cloud that no-one had the skill to dispel. The odious part was that Diana's dismissive 'they' had led Margaret to start thinking in the same way about the English. The slogans about Trinity kids, 'West Britons', 'snobbish', 'elitist', seemed justified. Any kind of chauvinism, or even nationalism, had for a long time now seemed very uncool. She had almost forgotten the jokes about Braggarty and the history lessons of Miss McCarthy, and if she thought about nationalist-minded people at all she saw them as zealots, probably rigidly Catholic, unsensual and, if male, either Pioneers or else footless most of the time.

But the casual slight, and the way no-one dealt with it openly, revealed how discourteously English people could still lord it, how much they presumed. She trusted her silence was punishment enough. The one she wanted to punish — and this was the upsetting, the puzzling part — was Christopher. She regarded the vapid Diana as of no account, but should he not have rebuked her on Margaret's behalf, if not on his own?

Afterwards she considered his poor-spiritedness in a different light. To her he had stressed his Irish connections, his savour of difference from the partly or wholly UK population of Trinity, like Geoffrey, whose father was a stockbroker in Surrey, Sue, whose parents were GPs in Bradford and Nigel, whose father's companies were registered in the Channel Islands. She found it slightly pathetic that Christopher had not swung everyone in the car by his authority, that he had not dared to give everyone the opportunity to behave gracefully and redeem the whole silly business. Aiming, as he claimed to be, above all at social success, he failed completely when he failed to dominate, to show his colours. She continued to trace the reasons: he probably always deferred to Nigel because Nigel was well-off and belonged automatically, without having to bother, to the right set, the social arbiters.

She pulled herself up. What was happening? The reasons she had found for his behaviour still seemed inadequate. Worse: it scared her to be finding him out this way.

On their next day all seemed to be well. She was happily explaining how her first few classes in the English Department had gone and about her plans for the year. She reflected later that she had done well not to tackle him about the Diana episode, or about the change she had detected in him. She shrank from being too undeceived about him. For the first time, she was sealing up feelings from him and (as best she could) from herself. On the sofa in his rooms, as she scanned his face, as she lay against his shoulder or his leg, she was using his presence, his animality: the hard mouth, the firm nape of his neck, the smell that came from tweeds and a faint suggestion of sweat, to annihilate all doubts, all misgivings. She was asking him, silently, to blinker her and to keep her blinkered.

Next day she had to check some references in Trinity Library and was crossing the front square when she saw, near the entrance to the Fellows' Garden, Christopher and Diana. Her shapely head was lying on his shoulder and they were holding hands. Even at that distance, Margaret could see she was tricked out with particular care. She carried out her task at the library, a cold pain and anger thickening inside her.

She met him at the front gate that night as usual. While he was signing her into his rooms, the thought crossed her mind that it would be for the last time. She managed to smile at the gnarled little porter in the jockey cap and tailed coat.

"Good evening."

"Evening, Miss."

They crossed the quad in silence. In his rooms, noticing her face, he asked. "What's up, darling?"

"I saw you this afternoon with Diana."

"Look, Margaret, dear, I've been meaning to tell you ever since I came back from London, but you've been so busy with your Finals."

"Tell me what?"

"That I'd been seeing Diana and that she arranged to be sent over to Dublin for a bit."

Margaret looked around the familiar room: at Nigel's pipe-rack, at the tea-caddy, the books, the cricket gear in the corner, the freshman's gowns hanging behind the door. She could hardly force out the words; she almost croaked: "You bastard. You've been two-timing me, and I trusted you."

"I wish you wouldn't sound so much like the broad in a bad gangster film," he said, trying to smile. Then more seriously, "I didn't mean to be such a heel, honestly, Margaret. We can go on seeing each other as friends if you want. I'd like that."

The awful thing was that she almost accepted. She almost said, "Yes, on any conditions, so long as I can be near you, look at you." She gained control only by summoning contempt for him.

"While you moon around that dizzy bird-witted shop assistant?"

She hoped the noun would sting him as much as the adjectives. It did.

"Oh, God, I can't stand brainy women," he said, "they complicate everything. Anyway, Diana is only doing that work to learn the business. She's setting up in her own salon in Bond Street next year."

Margaret caught a Number 7 bus home.

She put her chin on the dull silver bar that looped above the bus-seat in front. It made her head jangle. She wanted to

[118]

suck the cold, dirty metal.

V

THE COBH BACKDROP of run-down hotels and the church above could not be seen from the embarkation point under the shed.

An old man was saying good-bye to two girls of about Margaret's age. His eyes were deep-set in a bony face, the cloth of his jacket and trousers stiff as if they were too rarely worn to have been moulded by his limbs. On his creased brown neck the startlingly white collar sat loosely. The girls were not twins, but only a bare few months over the year separated them. Their grief was devastating in its quietness as each in turn they clung to him, sobbing wordlessly. They were dressed in a childish style with little fur collars on their coats, their hair long and wavy, their heels already chafed by the hard-looking shoes which had the air of last-minute purchases.

Margaret went on deck when the shore had already fallen some way behind. The girls were standing at the rail, waving vainly. She was prompted to go and talk to them, to ask what had brought them to this parting, seemingly so final, so bitter. But their distress enclosed, isolated them from well-meaning outsiders. Commonsense came to her aid: she reckoned that, later, they would be feeling more in the mood to talk and then she would talk to them.

But her commonsense arguments fell down. She never saw them once on the voyage to New York. Not on deck where anyone sitting in a deck-chair was comforted with bouillon; not at dinner where silver dishes were briskly chafed over blue flames; not at the cinema where Margaret happily watched films denied to Irish audiences; not on the floor, dancing in the middle of great tilts and rocks; not in the oak-panelled bar where Hungarian fiddlers sawed away over the heads of any couple having a drink; not around the huge supper tables, at the end of the day loaded with elaborately-presented, unappetising food. While passengers sampled the evening's amusements, the display was being mounted: swans sculpted in butter, castles sculpted in ice-cream, jellied moulds so coated (with mayonnaise or confectioner's cream), so garnished (with red pimentoes, anchovies, or glacé cherries) that it was hard to be sure whether, the disguise once penetrated, they would turn out to be meat, fish or dessert.

Time had, as always, to be filled in. Since ordinary pre-occupations were missing, new ones had to be found. So passengers spent their days eating or planning when or what to eat, playing games or planning when and what to play, doing themselves up, letting themselves go, taking each other out, or in, before their ordinary lives once again claimed them on the other side of the ocean.

At night in the smaller, glass-walled bar, Margaret saw men who held down modestly significant jobs, who worked with a photo of their wife and kids on the desk in front of them, make maladroit attempts to move their hips and mouths seductively as they raised their voices (seasoned by decades of cocktails and cigarettes) to say that they loved Paris every moment, every moment of the year. The piano, where a nondescript girl was hoisted up, was the heart of the bar as the bar was of the ship and the ship of the awesome black ocean, the awesome black sky. But even from this blackness ridiculous, vain, human bravery could sufficiently distract.

The day after they sighted dolphins the boat reached New York.

Margaret noticed the girls far down towards the end of the customs shed, near the exit to the bright, traffic-filled space where New York began.

"How come you're going there — it's a boys' school;" the official looked up from a scrutiny of Margaret's passport.

"Girls go to the Graduate School." Margaret flaunted her achievement.

In his crisply-pressed short-sleeved shirt, he looked jaded in the heat. "You're going to study English? Don't they speak good English in Ireland?" He made three syllables out of the last word.

"The best English there is."

"Good luck, Margaret."

From Donna's bed came an urgent whisper. "Don't move. I've dropped my contacts somewhere."

"If I don't move, how can I look for them? It's you who shouldn't move."

Donna had lost her contacts every three days on average since the beginning of term. But Margaret knew she was fortunate in her room-mate since first she had seen Donna, a rucksack on her back, long hair hanging behind, a carton balanced on her head, bringing the remainder of her stuff into the Residence.

Donna was fascinated by Catholicism. Brought up in a tepidly Episcopalian home, she fell upon Margaret with questions: why Catholics wouldn't limit their families, or divorce, how nuns dealt with their sexual feelings, why women couldn't go inside the altar rails during Mass. Margaret started to tell her about the loveliness of the gesture the priest made when he set his hands apart, but Donna wanted to hear something more dramatic — for instance, about Margaret's having once desired a priest and haunted his confessional. Margaret wanted to talk about how she felt as a Catholic among Protestants, a Protestant among Catholics. And Walter reading the *Book of Samuel*, and the damnation of the Rosenbergs, and the Coronation film and the paschal morning in Galway, and the stains on the ceiling and the Curé's honey, the nuns' Angelus and the marching workmen: how to explain any of that?

The half-basement kitchen was hushed, airless, with a tindery smell from the dried-out leaves still hanging. From time to time one of the big curvey fridges gave a sudden thump as Margaret tackled her first spell of kitchen duty. She had taken a roster with Donna but Kenzo, the elder of the two polite Japanese men, had offered to take Donna's place when she was called upon to act as usher at a Woolsley Hall concert.

He was a deft and fairly quiet worker. It seemed that he too loved bringing order out of the chaos that dinner sessions caused. The pair on kitchen duty had to run the dishwasher with saucepans only, clean down the tables, mop the floors, worktops and cookers. Little Australian Linda, bored by the diligence of her young husband who studied industrial chemistry late into the night, often came, her hair messy, her feet bare, for a chat and a snack from the fridge.

During the Depression stone-masons had been employed to embellish with Gothic ornamentation the university buildings. Everywhere carved stone figures caught the eye. Those on the Law Building were especially mocking: in the archivolts of the Wall Street entrance policemen were shown apprehending felons and judges sentencing them. A client in the shape of a goat handled his money bags and, above him, a parrot expounded the law. On Grove Street, near York, Law herself was shown blindfolded, helpless at the hands of a jester in cap and bells.

The library entrance on Wall Street had a carving of bookworms. In the light of latticed windows and huge chandeliers Margaret crossed the tessellated floors, up the aisles through the catalogues, towards the lofty issue desk. All the knowledge in the world awaited her as, soothed, she sought a niche to read till her head jerked forward with fatigue.

Mr Henry Wakefield's tiny, precise writing on fawn linen laid paper summoned Margaret to lunch at his house on Thanksgiving Day. His chauffer, Ettore, would call for her at ten o'clock. Margaret was curious to meet her benefactor: Mr Wakefield had provided the cash for her post-graduate study, through a fellowship that bore his name. She found herself curious also about the chauffeur, Ettore. Her expectations had to do with black eyes, maroon breeches, leggings, a small, hard pair of buttocks like those of the boys who worked in the pink Venetian Cafe, the first fish and chip shop to open in Ballsbridge.

But the young man who waited on the steps was tall and slim, his eyes the colour of the icy blue day, and he was wearing loose clothes of an old-fashioned cut. He conducted her to the elegant car.

She sat back on the soft, faintly crinkled leather seats, admiring the arm-rest, the cunningly-fitted walnut of the door and dashboard.

"What make of car is it?"

"A renovated 1936 Cadillac. I keep it in perfect condition for Mr Wakefield."

For weeks before Thanksgiving notices had appeared on the bulletin boards promising terrific company in return for rides back to Minnesota, Detroit, Grand Rapids, or Orange County and onwards to the thousands of smaller places that composed America. Only the foreign students (the Residence was full) and the sternly purposeful Graduate Students (who would stay in the library as long as any part of it was open and otherwise pillage its shelves in view of a long weekend) claimed the campus.

They left the city by a route unfamiliar to Margaret. The stretch of highway passed close to where, under the stilts of a huge flyover, a graveyard was trapped on a narrow, straggling island. She had a quick glimpse of headstones with little medallion photos, wreaths heaped up for removal. The Italian population of the city was proportionally the highest in the United States: many of them were buried there. She was led to a contemplation of Ettore.

The upper reaches of the harbour were fetid: barriers of railways and crumbling factories lined the highway. Beyond the dingy environs of the city stood long-established industries: arms, sewing machines, typewriters, corsets. Out in the valley, the hills were dramatic with crimson sumac, yellow maple and scarlet oak. Ettore drove fast and skillfully, and she watched his thin wrists. The farther they advanced into that country of poultry, tobacco and truck farmers, the more she wondered about so smoothly cosmopolitan a being.

"What part of Italy do you come from?"

"Sicily."

There was silence till he told her, "We'll be there in five minutes."

They first passed through a small village where the crisp white board church on the green was still the largest building, with the tiny gas station as the only other public place. In front of the church had once stood the stocks for the punishment of raillery or lewd song.

Among white trees, with a view of distant cow-pastures, stood Mr Henry Wakefield's house. Outside plain, strong and seemly, it overflowed inside with portraits, etchings, statuary, coins, bas-reliefs, enamels, miniatures, armour, bronzes, ivories, faience, pot-pourri jars, snuff-boxes, teapots, seals and rings: above all, it abounded in books and manuscripts, the spoils of many years of trips to Europe to acquire everything related to Horace Walpole that Mr Wakefield had been able to buy and move.

He greeted Margaret in the hall with "Welcome to Walpoleshire" while Ettore removed the car to neat yards at the side of the house. The hall opened into a huge library space, two storeys high, its upper shelves and the gallery accessible by a spiral staircase and numerous ladders.

Mr Wakefield sat with his back to the window, which

framed a scene of peaceful fields and railed paddocks. His hair and accent had the slight frost of a sound fruit, an apple or a pear from a northern garden. The meal began with clam chowder.

"The Connecticut Yankee version that we've always made in my family," he told Margaret. "It allows of neither tomatoes nor cream." Then turkey, bright vegetables of the pumpkin variety, a simple pie. The wizened little maid who had opened the door to Margaret and another, apparently identical, both in black dresses, white aprons and caps, served it all: Bridget and Mary Kate had left Roscommon, sailed west from Queenstown, and gone into service with the Wakefield family. Mr Wakefield remembered when they had had little more than bed and board. He had always found that the Irish made the best servants; it sounded as if Horace Walpole would have agreed.

For Mr Wakefield's water and for Margaret's orange juice the shaved ice was plentiful.

His ancestors had been among the first to make a landfall on the barren wind-whipped coast, to tame with work the rich land that had seemed to them unpeopled. Mr Wakefield too believed that he had been put into the world to do what the world required, to work at a warrantable calling. He believed in the power of events to show forth where the future lay. In the coincidence of the initials he shared with Horace Walpole he had discerned a pointer to his destiny. He began to tell Margaret about it.

"I've been going to London for the past thirty years to collect Walpoleana," he explained. "The war was a nuisance, it interrupted my searches. You see, Miss Hogan, I was convinced that there existed many more letters than had appeared in Mrs Paget Toynbee's edition of the *Corrrespondence*, and in the event I've been proved right."

They sat on, each pleased with the other. Mr Wakefield was very gentlemanly, and he found in Margaret the first Irish student who had as much as heard of Horace Walpole. The former Taoiseach who administered the fellowship at the Dublin end had sent out a succession of male law students, and for Mr Wakefield previous Thanksgiving lunches had been flat and formal.

Margaret's interest in the *Correspondence* was more than polite. She was not exactly a Walpolean but she had always loved the eighteenth century, or at least Pope and Swift, Frederick the Great and Rousseau, Mozart and Jefferson. The little Walpole factory kindled her curiosity. All was orderly: the catalogues, the bookshelves, the boxes of manuscripts, some not yet unpacked.

"On the Walpole empire the sun never sets. On average, a letter arrives every five to six days." She looked at the provenance: from Fife, from Hawaii, from Ibadan, Geneva, Bergen, Lima and Palermo letters had turned up.

"I was especially delighted to find out, following an advertisement in the 'agony column' of the *Times*, that a set of letters to Lady Ossory had survived. It was supposed by earlier editors that they had been burned in Ireland at the beginning of the twentieth century. Having acquired these, I can claim to have the original, or a copy, of almost every known scrap of the handwriting of H.W."

As Mr Wakefield explained more about the letters, how H.W. had regarded them as as an extension of conversation directed at posterity, how he found and if necessary replaced correspondents appropriate to the matter of the letters, whether on politics, antiquarianism, or social life, H.W. became clearer to Margaret.

She was thinking how delightful it would be to take a topic for her doctorate from the treasures assembled there. She saw herself, an apprentice to the humble task of the annotator, stalking private owners, elucidating niceties of style, distinguishing between abbreviations and contractions, the true inwardness of ibid., idem, op. and loc. cit. and c.f. It would, perhaps, fall to her to help explain small events or large: an outing to Vauxhall, the activities of Mme. du Deffand's garrulous and decrepit salon in the Convent of St Josephe, the execution of the Scottish rebel lords, the visit of the French spy and captain of dragoons who was adjudged by a jury in the Court of King's Bench to be a woman, a brush with the famous highwayman McLean, the affair of Admiral Byng, the obsequies of George II, the quarrel between Rousseau and Hume, the unhappy Chatterton business.

On her own small desk in a book-lined sanctuary Margaret could put a dish of stones from the New England countryside, epitomising her present profitable and plain existence: basically-dressed, clock-regulated, fair-minded, responsible, salad-eating, water-drinking. Her earnest industry would be unfailing of rewards.

They took a walk outside. Mr Wakefield wanted to show her where, the winter before, he had put up snow fences. He liked building dry-stone walls, too: he was always about improvement. In this corner of a New England valley his family had set themselves to the task of purging the shortcomings and vices of old England. Yet Mr Wakefield's words brought Margaret into a landscape of elegant and fanciful villas standing by rushy eyots where, out at Twickenham, H.W. had had as neighbours dowagers, dilettanti, retired generals, and opulent merchants.

"We lack only the nightingale here," he told her. Like H.W., he knew relief when his hay was cut and carted, delight when the squirrels came to be fed under his window. More wistfully, he acknowledged the contrast. "The countryside around Twickenham was more *riant*, of course, but the roads were infested with highwaymen, so it was difficult for H.W. to induce friends to dine with him. I don't have that problem."

Margaret looked back towards the house: Ettore, in a white jacket, was caught at a window of the annexe. When, finally, they turned in again, the light was at an end and he was gone.

They were finishing a light supper, served near the library fire, when Ettore came with the news that the car, exceptionally, was refusing to start and would require the attentions of a man from the garage who could not be contacted till morning.

"There's no remedy for it, Miss Hogan, you'll have to spend the night out here in Walpoleshire. You'd better ring the Residence and let them know. Perhaps you'd like to go for a ride tomorrow morning?" He looked questioningly at Ettore who shrugged.

"She could go out on Nimble, I suppose."

Mr Wakefield showed her the door in the middle of the gallery that connected with the landing and bedrooms. The traffic of the house went normally through the hall and up the main stairs.

The guest bedroom was furnished with odd items from Mr Wakefield's collection of eighteenth-century prints. When she finally lay down, tired but somehow unquiet, it was after prolonged prowling, prolonged perusal of gross and boisterous scenes: electioneering, duels, gin-shops, bedlam and brothels.

H.W. did not belong to the stout-waistcoated, fat beef and port eighteenth-century type. His gauzy essence like a gnome's, little, gouty, waspish, seemed present to her, spectral yet kindly.

She could not sleep. She was more awake than anyone else on earth. She could hear not only the clock that struck down in the hall but the dying embers dwindling in the grate of the library, not only the owl that hooted, was silent and hooted again, outside in the boughs but the leaves of the viriginia creeper that shifted in the breeze around her window, not only the sudden gust that rattled windows and banged a door but the faint kissing sounds of the bats as they jerked and zigzagged from the caves and back.

She slipped to the window just in time to see Ettore in a cream-coloured convertible turn into the entrance to the yard. Her first thought was about where, on this Thanksgiving night, he had been so late. But a more fundamental question remained. If he had a car, why had no-one suggested using it to bring her home? She went through the possibilities, the explanations, for Ettore's strange position in the household. He was Mr Wakefield's illegitimate son, conceived on a trip to Sicily, he was blackmailing Mr Wakefield, he was his lover, he was a penniless *principe* whom Mr Wakefield had collected like the other tropies he brought home every autumn.

She calculated in how many minutes he would reach and climb the stairs from the hall. Then she recalculated. He did not come. Suddenly launched beyond shame or prudence, she slipped through the door of the library gallery. Under her feet the gallery fell away to a void, at the bottom of which Ettore and Mr Wakefield moved in jerky sequence closer to the fire, closer to each other.

Ettore had thrown his overcoat across the large dictionary on its stand. His silk scarf still hung over his chest. He didn't remove it when Mr Wakefield's hand stretched inside his soft roomy shirt. Ettore's Valentino profile was sharp against the firelight, his gestures practised to please.

She could not catch their words, but she guessed at a strain between them. She knew that her Thanksgiving visit had contributed to driving Mr Wakefield from his bed to wait in his dressing-gown by the refuelled fire. Its light shone warmly on Ettore's golden shoulder, on Mr Wakefield's white one, but its heat died in the upper space before it reached her. She thought of the shocking portrait in which an exquisite masquerade costume had been joined to the face of the old H.W. So his carmine dressing-gown seemed to increase the symptoms of dilapidation in the diminished figure of Mr Wakefield.

Ludicrously placed above them like a deity, she could rather have wept like a fellow-creature to find how frail are the defences raised against passion, against sadness. To ponder that nothing was straight brought, gradually, gladness: the old man at his climacteric was still in the market for the bright, cruel Hollywood thing, still ravening for his youth.

It was a shock to waken with Ettore bending over her, as he placed a laden tray on a stand at the foot of her bed. He was wearing a white jacket fastened high around the throat like a steward on a transatlantic boat. She thought it most curious that he, not one of the maids, served her breakfast in bed.

"Eat while it's hot, you'll need plenty of energy for your

[131]

riding lesson," he said coolly, lifting the tray into her lap, brushing her breast with his sleeve. A bell, slightly muffled but very close, sounded.

"I must go, Mr Wakefield wants me." Looking at her with his bony smile, he left. She heard him open the door of what she was certain was the next-door room. Pushing aside the tray, ignoring for the moment the magnificent breakfast of scrambled eggs, bacon, rolls, preserves, a sort of white farina, coffee and orange juice, she pressed her ear to the fireplace, but though noises came from the next room they seemed damped down to murmurs.

Mary Kate was waxing floors in the hall and Bridget bringing up a basket of linen.

Mr Wakefield asked her to look at the four volumes of Chattertonia that he had just purchased. He described the contents. "H.W. collected and annotated all these pamphlets, attacking him for his part in occasioning the death of the juvenile hoaxer." It seemed that H.W.'s first letter to the young poet promised recognition and the possibility of fame, and so Chatterton was all the more stung by the tone of the second. He accused H.W. of being a cold, snobbish dilettante, and after his suicide his accusations were so widely believed that H.W. was held responsible for his death.

Margaret had heard of the episode: as Mr Wakefield told it, it captured her interest. She learned about the forged medievalism, the fifteenth century style scrambled together from eighteenth-century glossaries by the ingenious ex-ostler who, according to Mr Wakefield, was not the gentle ill-used poet defended by Wordsworth and Shelley, but acrimonious, spiteful and dishonest. Mr Wakefield contended that there was no evidence that starvation or penury had brought about Chatterton's suicide: he was suffering from venereal disease. Margaret approved that H.W.'s placid and orderly existence had been capsized by the intrusion of the forger's mask. Like the Bedlam retreat, it had served to release poets from the inhibitions of the neo-classical conscience.

After lunch they walked out to the yards. Mr Wakefield.

who had not in the past shown any difficulty about walking, gripped her arm, saying that he had trouble negotiating the cobbles. This morning he seemed at once more frail and more excited. After a few minutes his clutch on her arm began to bother her because she felt she couldn't change the angle at which she held her own arm. His pale skin was swept with blood and his eyes blinked rapidly.

Intermittent snortings and stampings sounded from the stableyard where Ettore was polishing up a stirrup-iron at the door of the little harness-room. He finished his task in a leisurely way, then fetched a glossy bay horse and a grey printed with silver marks like the impress of coins. Ettore was wearing a pair of fawn breeches and tall boots with a jumper. He carried a small crop with a dark leather thong. The grey was called Nimble, he told her, and she should pat its nose, exchange breaths with it, to make friends.

Bending down by the horse's side, he cupped his hands. "Go on, step on my hands."

She set one foot on the cradled hands and he gave her a leg up into the saddle. Aloft on what seemed a mountain of flesh, Margaret enjoyed the breathless flurry of being carried along, holding the thin inflexible reins, conscious of the cold slippery saddle, the freshness and strength of the horse under her.

They moved out into the paddock with Nimble on a leading-rein. After some time spent walking, Ettore told her to try 'rising to the trot'. Margaret had never dreamt of so serene and poetic an experience. This was what she wanted to do, on and on and on.

Remembering the Irish bank lent it more gusto. The double bank, as it was properly called, was the only jump in the RDS enclosure that didn't need to be built up by the men in brown overalls who were responsible for making up and trimming the jumps and repairing them if they were damaged. When the family went to the Horse Show, William spent a lot of time watching these brown figures because he wanted to have that job when he grew up, but Margaret loved rather to be sitting so as to see a rider and horse scramble over the double bank. It was a great wedge of green, like a blunt triangle, and someone on the radio had once described it as the Irish bank. The wrong name better conveyed the spirit of the thing.

Ettore taught her to keep her toes up, her hands down, her knees well stuck in, and to look out between Nimble's ears. They continued into the woods as a small repair truck came into the yard.

A mechanic bent into the opened bonnet of the Cadillac. She contrived to catch up with Ettore. "I heard you coming back last night." He looked back, reptilian, unperturbed.

They turned for the house. Margaret's thighs and buttocks were pulled and heavy. The sun was setting red and cold over the black hills and the slope of firm pastureland. Ettore showed her how to dismount: clear your feet from the stirrups, then turn around and slide down. He reached up and caught her around the waist. As she leaned against the deliciously sweaty neck of the horse Margaret was again aware of the flash of light at an upper window. Something shiny — and binoculars came at once into her mind — had caught the low-hanging sun. She noted which room it was: next to the one where she had been lodged the night before.

Margaret genuinely intended to take up Mr Wakefield's invitation and return soon to Walpoleshire. But her prospects of doing so seemed to decline with every week that passed. What had seemed in the first semester to be a manageable work schedule began to expand. She found it difficult to keep up occasional stints at concerts as an usher in her black formal and the vicious patent shoes, her hair in a neat pageboy.

She was allowed, in any case, to postpone the choice of subject for her thesis till the following year when she would have fewer required courses and be able to spend more time on independent study. The question of the H.W. correspondence was postponed, as was further investigation of the peculiarities of Mr Wakefield's *ménage*.

Margaret had long been a connoisseur of the smells of her own body. In Killiney or in the back garden at home the sun ripened the skin at the crook of her elbow and the back of her hand into a sharp fruity scent. The night smell, sampled by pulling the round neck of her pyjamas over her nose, was more general: a girdle, an aura of warmth in the chill of the bed. When reading or studying alone she sometimes quickly snatched a glimpse of balmy breasts and throat, caught the faint fume they gave off. She liked the contrast between the sticky patch of skin under her watch and the hand itself while it still carried a tonic smell of Lifebuoy soap. America had brought increased appreciation of the contrast. September had been hot, and the stir of her day left her by evening dewed with a sweatiness already slightly sour, which she relished before sweeping it away with mild fragrant water. She often squatted on the bathroom floor beforehand, so as to catch, fleetingly, the aroma of her gaping cunt, the trail that had filled her pants with a riotous life.

Beginning to dry herself, she gathered the thick towel and patted her outstretched arms and curving legs now renewed. The mirror's clouded surface showed an indistinct shape that became the professor, naked except for a Durex on his rearing cock. He touched her pink, damp body, the strands of hair on her forehead and neck.

"Kiss me quick."

The professor's name was Zak Holzappel, and Margaret and he made love together almost every day in his small apartment, showering before and after.

They became quite damp and savorous again as they explored the scents, nosing each other on the check rug that covered the bed. The apartment was as bare as a teenager's room.

"Did you bring this stuff from Cleveland, the first time you left home?"

She wondered too, if his parents had kept the bedroom of their bright only child just as he had left it, with high-school pennants and graduation photos, as well as his yarmulka, on the wall.

[135]

On their first afternoon, he had been, as he said, prepared. He tore open a tiny pack and pulled out a fine sheath of rubber like a fingerstall. The first one had been a sickly pink.

He plumbed her deeply as she lay, spread and parted under the sweet weight of his pudgy body, stroking his thinning hair, licking his full lips.

Zak was as jealous as he was randy: he mistrusted all the men students who lived in the 'crazy house', as he called the students' residence. He knew everyone by repute and enquired into the minutiae of daily life there on the hill out from the campus towards the city limits. Parties were common during the first semester.

"Kenzo and Mishuma gave us a feast the other night," she told him. They were lying together, touching gently and playfully. "Kenzo's wife sent him seaweed, rice cookies and saké. He played some of the old music he studies. He's nearly as old as you and he's got a family also."

"I don't give a fuck about his wife and his darling kids, his old music or his polite giggles."

When she explained about the kitchen duty, he muttered darkly, "Who do you pick as a partner?"

Mononucleiosis was the fashionable disease that year. She always thought it was called glandular fever, but Zak roared with laughter. "That's a really antique term."

Mono was contagious, passed on by kissing, and if Margaret was ever especially tired he would pretend to be suspicious.

Zak rarely came to the Residence to see for himself the cast of characters they so enjoyed gossiping about. Making a proper dinner of steak, salad and baked potatoes was for Margaret a change from cheese sandwiches and omelettes snatched at the kitchen table before going back to the bedroom or the library to finish assignments.

The first time she saw Zak very angry was when the Canadian geologist, Dave, had said in his hearing that they wanted to play Jews and Germans, only they didn't have enough Jews. The only Jews in the house were the Directors. They had a nice apartment, Chagall prints on the wall. Myron and

Deborah went to great lengths to explain that they were not at all orthodox: they had been drinking beer the first night Margaret spent in the Residence, though it was Hanakah. But at one Easter party Deborah had parodied the Crucifixion and later drafted everyone into a dance from Israel, arms linked, whirling in a circle.

Zak was disgusted when Margaret told him about the episode. "She is one of those loud, bossy, castrating Zionists: it's a type I've fought to escape from. They start by talking about their hope chest, they end by cutting off a guy's balls."

Margaret found that Myron was a bit of a bore, with his tuba and his engineering studies.

"He made his mother happy anyway, being accepted here," Zak said another time.

"So did I, make my mother happy, I mean," Margaret said. "I bet you did too."

"You're damned right I did," he answered. "It was the top of the mountain for her and my dad."

His father worked in a garment business, having started in the sweatshops of the East Side and progressed to the ownership of a small factory in Cleveland. He had rarely taken holidays. After the old mother died Zak's mother gave up making the puddings of noodles and oil pastry they had brought from the black Austrian villages where they had been *Ratenjuden*, 'instalment Jews' selling trinkets and clothes on payday to the families of factory workers.

Zak's mother was always busy over goulash, blintzes and streudels, always wanting to feed people, but then also taking Zak on her lap to hold him, smooth his hair when, determined to come out on top of his class, the tiny boy worked on maths exercises late into the night.

The dentist he went to used to say, "I see from the paper you win all the prizes at school."

There wasn't a job Zak hadn't accepted. He ran the local swimming-pool, waited at table, answered emergency calls at night in the American Automobile Club. He had studied at Cornell and Berkeley before coming east for his doctorate. He had become an associate professor at twenty-three. From the hectic years he had kept the capacity to work long hours, early or late. He often rang Margaret at eight o'clock, having been at his desk at the lab for hours. He snatched a nap on the rug in the apartment after Margaret had left, and then went back to work till eleven or later.

She kneaded his hips and buttocks, which were thickened with pads of flesh. He was her true companion: not only abrasive and funny but enabling her to cut adrift from her earlier life. He glanced without interest at a card from Dublin: he could not distinguish Clery's from the GPO and she had no need to tell him.

The night she was vomiting at his friend Marcia's house, after the green peppers she had munched in the kitchen, the lethal punch which she had too rashly tried, he held his cool hand across her forehead, reassuring, while she looked through streaming eyes at the little packet of birth control pills on the shelf nearby. Marcia came in and, simpering at him, put them away.

Though Zak had always a good stock of condoms, he mentioned further precautions to Margaret. "It's better if you take care of it. I'll organise some pills for you."

"Are they legal?"

"They will be soon, I hope. Marcia's just trying to make some sort of bravado thing out of it. The Planned Parenthood Federation is to sue the State to have the law changed. The trouble is, it's a strong Catholic state because of the Italians."

He kissed her as if he would drain her dry.

Sometimes Zak was blissfully weary from playing basketball. Up on the fifth floor of the gym, where he often went on the spur of the moment, improvised games between 'shirts' and 'skins' took place. The competition was Darwinian, he told her, and she imagined him, his eyes softened to a myopic stare with his glasses off, sweating freely from the effort, as there with her on the rug, growing heavy against his arm, while she whispered nonsense, tipping his ear with her lips.

"Why is it that Jews answer one question with another?"

"Why not?" he murmured, almost asleep.

One smoky November evening, she told him, "I'll go early, I want to catch the vegetable man."

"So now it's the vegetable man," he stormed. "I've said that no-one makes assignations with you except me. Why can't you buy plastic-wrapped stuff at the supermarket like everyone else?"

She laughed, explaining about the van, fragrant and dim inside, with shelves full of the most beautiful things she had ever seen: yellow peppers, broccoli, nectarines. That evening hour pleased her too: Australian Linda was often only half-dressed but did at least rouse herself once the long afternoon, broken only by the mailman's visit, was over.

The huge ellipse of the Bowl was built to solicit vast crowds in a simpler and more robust era when big-time football, with career coaching and frenzied recruiting, had begun.

The weekend of the Princeton game Donna's younger sister, a junior at Smith, was coming. On their way to the Bowl, Margaret and Donna crossed Parking Lot B. Parking Lot B was what was called a Pass Lot. Passes were granted to the oldest and most select of the alumni who were still active and could exert pull. To the people in Parking Lot B the game was almost incidental. They were greeting their friends, expecting to find the same people parked in the same places from one game to the next preparing for the out-door picnics that were known as tail-gating. Wide thermos jugs, upright cases of bottles and picnic baskets stood on the jutting tail-gates of the cars. Oak planks held cheese and crackers, stuffed clams in steamers, sweet and sour hot dogs in large crockery jars. The well-ordered rite had here its appointed ground. A fine-profiled old lady was laying out provisions in the bitter wind. Some men in expensive suits were kicking a kid's football around on the sparse grass. They seemed addicted to nicknames.

"Good old Gunboat — he always comes in a fire-engine."

"Did you hear that Smokey has become a member of the Paths and Trails commission — property owners and the general public have to be protected from the nature nuts."

[139]

"Anyone know anything about Cobbles?"

"Well, you have to remember Cobbles reached the mystic 75, just last month. He keeps a substantial interest in the hardboard factory at Salonica and he never misses a Class Reunion."

The old lady had grown up with the midwinter ritual. She was the daughter, wife and mother of alumni. In her young days the bar had always been located behind the driver's seat.

It had been -15° for three days, and the wind-chill factor was 40° F. From the raked terraces of the Bowl, they could see the Precision Marching Band going through some phallic routines to warm up the crowd before the game began.

A fellow standing on Donna's left grinned. "There'll be protests: there always are, to the President of the university, the *Daily News*, the Daughters of the American Revolution."

"Do the protests have any effect?"

"Are you British or something? No, they certainly have no effect on the band's performance, but the protesters really enjoy dwelling on the workings of minds so deep in the gutter, as they say."

The people watching the game wore blonde clothes. Both men and women had fur coats, cashmere scarves and brogue-type shoes. Some cheerful faculty wives weathered the chill in Peck and Peck houndstooth check suits and old sheared racoon coats.

Donna could not easily explain what was going on. Margaret found the action very scrappy. She could make little of the strange barked signals, the significance of the brutal formation known as a flying wedge. She supposed that the undergraduates brought their girls to the game to induce in them a mood of excitement at the contemplation of bulbous calves, waists shrunk by contrast with mammoth shoulders and biceps. She found herself watching the spectators more than the players. Young girls, brought down from Vassar or Smith for the weekend, talked, yawned, waved to distant specks of friends and occasionally looked in the programme to see who Number 91 was.

By night the warm-up, begun in the Bowl, would be completed. By night the visiting girls would be jerking off the football heroes and their supporters.

Donna had described to Margaret what the weekends were like. "After the game our dates bring us back to the dorms, to the gin bottle and the can of grapefruit juice. We go to Mrs Smith's boarding house and chat and giggle on the beds with our feet up on the posts, cold cream on our faces. Gardenias arrive in florists' boxes. No-one who is anyone arrives before the intermission, so we have plenty of time to fit ourselves into strapless dresses stiffened with whalebones, asking one another to pin us up in the back. It's the rule to let the boy wait – it shows you are not eager."

The Prom orchestras all sounded alike: probably because they were all composed of the same musicians, a pool of part-timers, hired at a kind of shape-up in New York the previous Wednesday at the Roseland. The young couples glided, turned, walked or dipped till 'Goodnight Sweetheart' told them the end had come. In the morning they told Mrs Smith how comfortable the beds had been. Their dates took them to the station and they waved as long as they could see them though they had already run out of things to say.

Donna also told her what had happened to one girl at the hands of some students at the Law School. They smuggled her into the dorm, blindfolded her, put a peeled banana in her hand and twirled her in a circle, first quite noiselessly, later to the accompaniment of a strange clamour.

A circular space on the floor of the laboratory was marked off in squares and surrounded by a mesh barrier. The area was brightly illuminated by neon. Above it a number of loud-speakers produced a common level of noise, a sibilance that to Margaret was both unfamiliar and disconcerting. It was something like a waterfall or an escape of gas but had no variation, so that the ear could detect no pattern. The rat above whose innocent head the noise was pouring cowered at one side of the circular space, his whiskers trembling, otherwise quite rigid, frozen with fright. Every time his papery sides contracted, a small black fecal bolus dropped behind him and a puddle on the squares enlarged. Each time either event occurred the assistant, a young man with an Abe Lincoln beard and no moustache, made a note on a clipboard ruled in columns.

"O.K. Norm," Zak called. "You can take him out. I'm bringing in one of the group B ones now."

To Margaret, on her first visit to the lab, the group B rat looked identical to the first one, which she presumed was group A. He too — though of course she could not be sure of its sex — was pure white with large ear-lobes of an upsetting flesh pink and a bald, almost scaly tail. Zak put him into the circular space just as Norm removed the first one, whom she understood to be called Harold.

The second rat was called Stanley. He was much more active than Harold had been. He ran round the area, and every time he crossed a line Norm ticked a different column of the record sheet. Though the 'open field' as it was euphemistically called contained nothing whatever, Stanley sniffed and explored it quite freely. He deposited occasional boluses, but much fewer than Harold.

"Do you want to try the noiseless condition?" suggested Zak, and Stanley was again replaced by Harold, who seemed only a little less nervous when the noise was turned off. Norm had connected lines on a graph after each session, which was meticulously timed to last exactly ten minutes. The automatic timer recorded each event: line-crossing, defecation or urination.

When both rats had been run in the noiseless condition it was lunch time. They moved along the corridor, where an open door revealed a tank of jelly-fish. They were joined by some more of the graduate students: Hub and Wes and Rod and Mel: did any of them have more than one syllable in their name, she wondered. Like Norm, they were working on Zak's major research project, but they were also running smaller projects of their own with titles like 'The Ontogeny of Reactivity to Dipsogenic Stimuli'.

Before he left the lab for the day, Zak supervised the substitution of two more rats, Frederick and Nathan, one from each group, for testing in both conditions.

"What is the difference between group A and group B?" Margaret asked.

"Basically, group A were brought up without any stress when they were infants and group B were mildly stressed during the same period."

"What do you mean by mild stress: not that fearful noise back there?"

"No, of course not. We might give them very weak electric shocks, or else handle them. For an infant rat these would be mildly stressful experiences. Our hypothesis is that rats given this type of treatment will cope better with major stress, like the white noise and the open field, than rats not so treated. You noticed that Stanley produced fewer fecal boluses than Harold. We use defecation as an operational definition of fear. Also, Stanley showed much more active behaviour, exploration of the space, and this supports our hypothesis that the mild stress he experienced as an infant has helped him to adjust more appropriately to the major stress. His behaviour is quite integrated whereas Harold just goes to pieces."

"Why are they so scared of the open field?"

"Rats are accustomed to living in dark, confined spaces and they are generally emotional when they are placed in an open space. Their fear behaviour is exactly the same as humans display: during battle, for instance, most soldiers piss and many of them shit too in their pants."

Margaret found the science students more enthusiastic, more innocent almost, about their work than her classmates, who felt it expected of them to shrug off much deep personal involvement. After hearing the beaming Hub talk about the beautiful data he got when he worked on jelly-fish (he left only a narrow bridge of tissue connecting one half of their bodies to the other, making various patterns of cuts on their bells: spokes, spirals, random gashes, and noted how nonetheless the swimming beat continued and spread) she hardly knew how to introduce her own work.

Zak's five year old son, Noah, came for his quarterly visit. He was a self-possessed child, not good-looking but with thick black lashes. As they walked around the grass-ringed courtyards where Zak and Margaret had gone to hear jazz three nights before, he asked her to lift him onto the wall. He was spidery in build, a light burden, but as she held him close, momentarily, she was enchanted by the scent of his hair.

The break-in at the lab came almost at the end of the year. Margaret had fallen asleep over her last term paper the night before and was dull when Zak rang her at 7.30. But he showed no interest in her tiredness: he had just been informed that vandals had entered the lab, breaking computers and other stuff and, worst of all, letting the rats escape and draining the jelly-fish tank. This with 14,000 invitations already sent to alumni to visit the lab during Open House Weekend, then twenty-four hours away.

She didn't dare ask how it had happened: he told her anyway. "The fucking hall was waxed in anticipation of Open Day. The fucking janitor left the fucking ground floor window open to air the place, and the marauders came through there. But the worst was that the fucking bursary boy had neglected to lock up the fucking rats' living quarters securely."

The only crime on campus Margaret had heard of up to then was the business of the two defrocked priests of the Eastern Rite of the Greek Orthodox Church. As clergymen they were permitted full access to the stacks and had taken a rare atlas. The theft was discovered only when a San Francisco book dealer tried to sell the atlas back to the library. The two had plea-bargained and received suspended sentences.

But though the students rarely thought about it, the university stood on the border of two worlds, as if it were possible to avoid them coming into too much contact. In the evenings shoe-shine boys came to the corner of Elm Street from the quarters where pink Cadillacs were parked in front of shabby porches and the Stars and Stripes rarely hung. Was it assumed that they wouldn't notice they hadn't got what the students had, that they wouldn't care?

Margaret knew how serious the escape of the rats was, especially as the project had been close to completion. She went to help Hub and Norm and Mel and Lou and Rod to try and locate Nathan and Frederick and Harold and Stanley and the other rats.

None of them was ever seen again. Not being as street-wise as the kids who had let them out, they had, presumably, perished, taking with them, in their enlarged or otherwise adrenal glands, the evidence about stress and coping that Zak had patiently accumulated for so long. As she left the lab, the hapless janitor was dumping a bucket of jelly-fish, maimed and whole doubtlessly now mingled in a mess of life-stuff as he started to clean the empty tank.

Margaret's trip into the interior began with a train journey to Newark. She had purposely not informed the League people about the exact time of her arrival. After the busy last few weeks of courses she wanted some time that would be a kind of blank before going through with the reception by the Mayor, the presentation of a key to the city for Mr de Valera, and afterwards the League's own reception and Fourth of July picnic, at which she was to receive the St Colmcille award for travel in the United States. Zak was teaching a summer semester out in New Mexico, and Margaret hoped to join him there later. She longed to see the candy desert colours, the harsh empty sky.

The bellboy looked about sixty. He demonstrated how the complex lock on the hotel bedroom door worked and stressed that she should always look out through a kind of spy-hole before opening it.

"Where are you from, anyway, Greece?" was his final quip.

The heat of the city was rising from the streets and the air was fusty though it was still early in the day. Margaret lay on the bed in her slip and looked around. The room had everything she needed: she rejoiced. The furniture was cheap and impersonal: a closet, a little stand where the porter had put her case, a TV on the dressing table, its antennae in a wide V; and she found the Gideon Bible beside her bed. Outside, a street of dance-parlours and reducing salons, the refuse of the naive and desperate, where shops sold blackhead squeezers and stiff pats of joke vomit. The window didn't open because of the air-conditioning, a noisy box fitted to the window sill. She rejoiced in the non-ness of the place, in her own freedom to drift, to light out. Huck Finn's territory, Whitman's road, Crane's bridge: she could take it or leave it.

Opening the closet, she found a black bag. Seemingly very full, it put her in mind of a quarrel, a flight, a change of identity or worse. Suddenly, puzzlingly angry, she called the porter and had him remove it.

The late movie on tv was *The Quiet Man*. Dada had been down in County Mayo for the shooting of that film, she remembered, though exactly what had brought him there, besides the prospect of spending an enjoyable few weeks, she never knew. The events seemed remote and ridiculous, especially when Maureen O'Hara's dowry was thrown into the furnace. Utterly weary, she half watched John Wayne's big boring face, half read the New Testament. After a restless night she wakened with the Bible still in her hands, the screen now ill-adjusted, a flickering succession of lines.

Between sleep and waking, she hunted wildly on the closet floor for the piece of paper that had been roughly pinned, she was sure of it, to the black bag.

After such an awakening, she was glad to meet the League people and to be escorted. The Secretary, Kathleen, was plain, with hair hooked over her ears, upswept rhinestone-trimmed glasses, and a long straight skirt. Little older than Margaret herself, she seemed already a spinster, full of shy enthusiasm.

There was nothing shy about Mr D'Angelo, whose office was in the penthouse of City Hall. Accompanied by Kathleen, Margaret was taken up in a huge lift panelled in fumed walnut, then through offices where three secretaries conducted them in relays into the private office. The Mayor's suit matched his rippling silver hair. His handshake enfolded Margaret like his practised smile that came both from his chocolate coloured eyes and his well-maintained teeth.

Wearing a look of seriousness that had no object, he delivered a little speech about Mr de Valera and how honoured his name was in the United States. He next made the presentation, first slipping his fingers under the ledge around his huge walnut desk. At his signal from a hidden bell there emerged from the secretary's office photographers, their cameras aimed, to record the occasion. From the Mayor's hands Margaret took the key, bare of box or case. It lay among the blouses and slips in her suitcase till she went home.

The Fourth of July picnic, held in the garden of a retired judge whose four sisters still lived in Castlebar, was to be very informal, and the evening air was stuffy, looming. Margaret was glad she had worn a halter neck and shorts. After a welcome from Monsignor O'Hara, President of the League, and the introduction of the students who hoped to travel the following year to Dublin and the Yeats Summer School, the Irish airs began to sound from loudspeakers, a dancing display was given, and the food was handed around by members of the Daughters of Erin.

People began to talk of politics and the coming election. Margaret was surprised to hear how many of these Irish supported Nixon. On this feast of their Independence, they sided more strongly with the rural Protestant than the urban Catholic. It seemed important to be as American as everybody else, to repudiate Europe and the past.

"Kennedy sounds kinda soft on niggers."

"Ike's record is good enough for me."

"Remember how Nixon turned up evidence about the Reds in the State Department way back when he was working for that Congressman?"

Margaret couldn't follow and so lost interest in the conversation about a microfilm being hidden in a pumpkin on someone's porch. She took a bite of pretzel, tasting with pleasure the twisted knot of hard-baked dough sprinkled with large glinting flecks of salt. She suddenly felt a parting, a snapping, and found among the softened pretzel in her mouth part of a molar. Though there was no pain, the episode put her out.

On the edge of the picnic there had been a little flurry of excitement, and she noticed Kathleen walking quickly towards the house as if she had been summoned with urgency.

"We have to pour money into research, to close the missile gap, to draw ahead of the Soviets, keep communism out of our hemisphere."

On the evening before the picnic, just as Margaret had reached the hotel, a series of events had begun in Dublin which she was to piece together only later. Her father Patrick had developed the kind of bad turn that had been, till then, unusual in his case: a coma resulting from too little rather than too much insulin. Either his requirement for insulin had increased or its effectiveness had decreased or his metabolism had simply gone out of control. The end products of the oxidization of fat accumulated in his blood so that the excessive ketone bodies gave his breath the smell of nail-varnish remover. When Dutch and Mama had noticed his deep and laboured breathing, his drowsiness and nausea, they tested for acetone and found that the paper showed suddenly a deep purple, indicating a dangerously high level. A further dose of insulin had left it still at at a fairly deep purple and they rang the specialist. He advised them to call an ambulance and bring him into Vincent's Hospital. When the attendants struggled down the stairs Dutch could not bear to stand in the hall and watch, as she had done when the RIC had brought him down the same stairs on the night of his arrest so long before. The severance was too extreme, too final: she was convinced he would never come back. It was of no avail to remind herself that she had thought the same in 1920, or that he had been taken half-conscious to hospital before.

Dutch had been anxious to lift all trouble from him, to shield and spare him as if he was too fine, too pure to know the badness of the world. She felt it was more fitting that she have transaction with it. Yet at this supreme moment she had to hide, to run from so much sadness. She had intruded on the two of them, on him and his wife, for most of their married life. At this moment she left them alone, though it would have been hard to know on whose account she was doing it. There was in any case something touchingly human, satisfying even, in the gesture, the shutting of the breakfast room door on the straining figures with the slung canvas chair.

Mama was strangely calm when she came down the main steps of Vincent's and looked around at the sparse traffic of a Tuesday at eight a.m. An old woman was shouting shrilly at the closed door of Loreto Hall. She wore a hat and her stained lisle stockings were twisted on her thin legs. On each foot they were snagged by a dirty thickened toenail. Under her arm she clutched a paper-wrapped bundle. The colours of the trees in the Green — the colours of high summer in Ireland — were somehow lurid and grim, though the day had come with a high, light blue sky.

A nurse had given Mama a cup of tea in the little office along the corridor from the ward where she had stayed all night. She now wanted to walk in the Green before she began making the phone calls — to Dutch, who had last rung about six, to Margaret in America, to the Hogans in Carlow, to relatives who could attend to what were called the arrangements. She had always summoned a kind of wild strength in the teeth of a crisis but now, though she thought she could still count on it, she also thought that she would never need it again. She anticipated the outcry of grief from many people: from little Mary, from poor William and Margaret, from Dutch who, she thought scornfully, had flinched from the ordeal, had left her to face alone the semi-private bed shut off with flowered screens, the ever-rising levels of acetone and sugar in Patrick's blood that no dosage of insulin could by then reduce, the thirst, the ketosis that showed how he was burning up, carried away from her by a squall of noisy breathing.

Though he was not of an age to die, there was a good gap of years between them and she was now only forty. She had been a widow of half an hour when, on returning to the hospital, she insisted on ringing Dutch herself and refused the nun's offer to do so.

Though she had brought a small suitcase with Patrick's things, she was upset to find they had been put into a large black bag which was left leaning against the wall of the office with his name affixed.

Kathleen prepared Margaret for the news that awaited her on the telephone inside. Margaret kept probing the jagged ruin of tooth with her tongue: its contours were beginning to become as familiar as they had been in its whole state.

With everything known and settled she came back outside. The party was hushed. Most people gathered around the Monsignor. He announced that he would, exceptionally, schedule a Mass for the next morning in the main Irish church so that friends of the League could pay their respects, condole with Margaret before she left on the first stage of her journey back to Dublin for the funeral.

Ever practical, Kathleen explained that Margaret could, of course, keep the full amount of the grant intended for travel in the United States. "We'll see you back here again, Margaret, that's for sure." Margaret noticed a half-eaten cob of corn, lipstick-stained, on a paper plate nearby.

Everything about Monsignor O'Hara was shiny: his steel-rimmed glasses, his close-packed, perfect teeth, the shot hues of his scarlet satin sash that was slightly raised by his ample stomach and clashed with the crimson piping of his soutane. In his sermon he took advantage of the poignance of the occasion and of the large attendance to touch upon themes which were always close to his heart. He spoke of patriotism, of devotion to the American way of life and to the parochial schools. He expressed a hope that the congregation would give whole-heartedly in support of these schools which passed on, intact, the repository of Catholic doctrine and practice.

He spoke also of Ireland: a land where the smile had always masked the tear, poor in everything but the faith and the blessing of God, resigned to His will.

He had already promised Margaret that he would wear at this Mass the pure gold vestments that he kept for special occasions. Liturgically speaking, gold (trimmed with green silk) seemed an odd choice for a Mass in honour of one recently deceased. Afterwards, the Monsignor beckoned her over to the vestry.

"I especially wanted you to see them," he beamed.

Margaret gathered up the end of the chasuble in her hands. At close quarters it was hard, heavy and cold, even more disagreeable than it had looked on the altar.

"I have to keep them locked in a safe," he explained. "They're worth thousands of dollars."

In the hushed voice that, since the day before, everyone was using to her, Kathleen told Margaret that her cousin Martin was waiting to see her. He had, presumably, been notified by Dutch and arrived before the Mass was over.

Her image of cousin Martin was still that of the sailor whose photo had been for so long on Dutch's mantelpiece: a cupcake hat, a knotted tie at the open neck; the youthfulness and the uniform somehow redeeming his undistinguished appearance. But the smallish, sagging man who was drinking coffee with her had a hearing aid, thick glasses and false teeth that slipped. He told her a lot about long-dead relations, especially his mother, the Aunt Gretta who used to join her name to his on the Christmas cards. Only when he spoke of his duodenum and his heart ailment did he become animated. When they said goodbye in the street the sunshine showed up his big pallid face, his crêpe-like hands.

Margaret sat on the bed, not yet removed, in which Patrick had sunk into the final coma. She was staring at the dressing-table with its pattern like drifts of smoke, its round mirror that had always seemed bigger and finer than those in the neighbours' front windows, bevelled three-panelled rectangles.

"Wasn't it very good of Martin to go and see you? It

pleased Dutch a lot." Mama was sorting through drawers as she spoke.

Margaret still had the awkward feeling of being out of scale with her surroundings: the landscape had shrunk, the trees were smaller, the roads shorter than she remembered; and the room that had once glowed now seemed cluttered and dusty, the tops of the wardrobes loaded with Patrick's things. Other people's goodness didn't count. Margaret was appalled at the prospect of losing him in all the talk, in all the sifting of his belongings, of papers with his fine copperplate writing. She held it against him that he had died when she needed him, before she had been his friend. She demanded to hear from Mama the inside story, the dope, on what had been glanced over, murmured away: the Ballykinlar interlude, the wound on his leg, their meeting, courtship and early marriage.

"Was that all before you knew him, all that political stuff?" She had to sound, to ransack sadly wounded hearts, including her own. She knew that otherwise the lie would curdle. Like the wardrobes, now small and dull, the reality would be diminished.

"Yes, he was very young at the time. He wasn't cute like the others, getting good jobs out of it."

Margaret knew then that Patrick was really dead since he was being fabricated, made over, pressed into service, transformed into a dummy. His essence was fading fast, like the distinctive smell from his clothes. His old friend, Jim, was downstairs, leading the conversation as he thought was correct onto neutral topics. Dutch had mentioned seeing the Earl coming out of Mass at Clarendon Street. Jim was able to tell her more, to tell them all more.

"He's a daily communicant and a member of the Third Order. A very distinguished looking man. There's a little story about his conversion. When he was thinking about becoming a Catholic a friend of his, a Protestant Minister, was very alarmed and took him on a trip to South America. He wanted to show the Earl how backward Catholic countries were compared with Protestant."

"But that didn't put the Earl off in the least," Margaret

broke in.

"That's right — how did you know?" Jim was slightly huffed that the end of his story had been anticipated, and not perhaps in the words he would have used. "Well, his friend's well-meant effort failed," he continued lamely.

If the Earl had wanted good works and social leadership he'd have stayed in the religion he was born into. What he wanted was a thrill, a whiff of barbarism. He had simply lapped up all the disreputable aspects of Catholicism: the capacity for double-think, the arrogance.

The presentation of the key to President de Valera seemed to be a matter of little significance either to the President's staff or to Margaret. Eventually she went through channels to arrange it. She could hardly do otherwise since she had been entrusted with the key, and besides, it seemed oddly appropriate, having the right quality of pointlessness for the weeks after Dada's funeral. If she secured the President's autograph Dutch would be pleased, she thought, and so she brought along Corkery's *The Hidden Ireland*, which had been her last prize at school, the day she went up to the Park for her eleven o'clock appointment. As she was taking the Mayor's key out of her pocket to show the President's Secretary who had welcomed her to the Aras, it slipped from her fingers and, missing the mat by about an inch, fell on the flags of the step. Some of the decorative scroll-work from the top broke off. The broken edge revealed pale clayey stuff that reminded Margaret of the nut-crackers they had bought anew every Hallowe'en because an almond or brazil nut had proved too hard. That the key to the city of Newark was also made from a sort of pig-iron somehow discharged her from the blame of having broken it. It would probably have broken sooner or later anyway.

The President's Secretary, a formally-dressed, serious-looking man with bushy eyebrows, high cheek-bones and a long upper lip, tried to reassure Margaret.

"Sure, now, there's only a little bit broken. It could have

been worse." Back in Ireland, Margaret was noticing how much the edge was taken off events by soft answers. "The President is very understanding," he was saying.

"The President is also blind," she thought, remembering the talk at home about the eye operations. As if he had read her mind the Secretary explained that the specialists in Utrecht had been able to maintain only a measure of peripheral vision and the ability to determine large objects.

Then all at once she was being introduced, in Irish, by the Secretary who left them alone in a ground-floor room with long windows. On that airless, expectant July day the whole Park looked like a mass of sullen green, colour without form. The furnishings in the room were undifferentiated too: they seemed to suck in the light, to mop it up. She looked at the President. He wore on his lapel the little embroidered ring, the symbolical fáinne signifying his willingness to speak Irish with anyone who spoke it with him. His handshake was firm and she found the way he took out a fountain pen and signed in a legible and stylish hand the book she opened in front of him impressive.

But his voice was the voice of an old Christian Brother as he talked to her of her stay in America. To her discomfort, he asked if people in America were concerned about partition.

"The unity of our country is the most urgent question. We should be ashamed to let a foreign power hold the Six Counties."

He visited his private chapel as often as five times a day. "I'm praying to God every day for that intention. The division of our country is a heartbreak. The American people feel it. It will be the great question over the next decades."

She believed, she knew he was wrong. Like the fáinne, it was symbolical. Once, the ground where he had moved easily was the formula, mathematical or constitutional, the circuitry, the complicated semantic reservations. Now it was the cliché, the tired repetition of his shibboleth.

Looking at him she remembered the simplicity of blind faces she had seen. With the sandals which, she understood, were his preferred foot-wear, his occasional outbursts of seminarian humour (he had chuckled when he told her 'Sweet is the life of the scholar') and now his divination of the future, Dev was as close to St Colmcille as she ever expected or wanted to approach. His stillness enclosed so much: the milk churns of Bruree, the North Circular Road Irish lessons, the Rotunda Rink recruitment, the battle at the bakery, the little jokes in Latin and Irish that prepared his springing from Lincoln Jail, the New York bond issue, the enlistment as a private, the tortuous decision to take the oath, the guardian of the country's neutrality, the pilgrim to the Western Isles recording Gaelic speakers.

But the inmost of the concentric circles of his mind were the suburbs around Blackrock, the location of many religious houses, in one of which he had begun his teaching career, and where now, increasingly, there were old comrades to visit in nursing homes.

Margaret didn't tell him that Dada had benefited from the rigged exams in clerkship that Dev had set for those who served in the National Movement, that he had experienced life on the run, that Dutch had marched past his reviewing platform at the GPO wearing a tin hat and a grey ARP uniform and had had his picture on the pink wall of her bedroom, admiring not only his unbending features but the touch of Latin glamour in his dark eyes and Spanish name. He had shepherded Ireland through the Arcady of the Emergency: clamps of turf in the Phoenix Park, brown bread, bicycles and gatherings around the radio sets which spoke of the affliction of Europe.

When she understood from the Secretary that the meeting should end Margaret expected to be treated to tea or to a conducted tour of the premises. But having spent, at most, twenty-five minutes at the Aras, she found herself again at the gate, being waved through by the guard with the revolver and the military policeman.

On O'Connell Street rain was beginning to fall. The Ireland Dev had made was all around and Margaret didn't need to look at his signature on the fly-leaf of the school prize book to know that he was real, the dadó who had presided over the pupillage of Ireland, left plain and misunderstood.

But, as she now saw, understanding was supreme. She had to understand it, the world that was unpeeling itself as she watched, or else hate it. Its sweetness would not defeat her.

Margaret moved into Dutch's bedroom that summer. Dutch had taken the pictures to her new flat in Dun Laoghaire, but their marks still ghosted the pink walls.

Margaret sat on the sill, as her mother had once done, her back to the open window so as to rub the panes. Across the dumb greens of the gardens came a distant, dreamlike sound — the hooter of the Swastika Laundry was calling the workers back after lunch along Shelbourne Road.